VAMPYRE CRYPT

CANDY RAE

DEDICATION

Vampyre Crypt is dedicated to the memory of my mother. She was absolutely terrified of those old, flickering, black and white vampire horror films, and would run from the room.

AUTHOR'S NOTE

Vampyre Crypt is written in what is known as Britannic, or British English but with a Scottish flavour, the occurrence of Lallans, or Lowland Scots being the most predominant. There are spelling and pronunciation differences between Lallans/Lowland Scots and the different dialects and versions of English as written and spoken in other parts of our wonderful, diverse world.

As well as English, the Faie speak Cuetiachtli, the Old Tongue, which is a mix of English, Lowland Scots, and Scottish Gaelic, together with some other languages, primarily Russian and German. For the purpose of this story, the Faie and the other races and kindred speak the same as the author, which is rather handy otherwise no one but she would be able to make sense of large chunks of this book.

THE MULTIVERSE MUDDLE

VAMPYRE CRYPT - Bhampair Làrach Todhlacaidh
FAIE CASTLE - Caisteal Na Sìobhragan
SURTR CHASM - Surtr Glomhais
DEMON CITADEL - Deamhain Daingneachd

Cover Artwork by Harri Crawford

BOOKS BY CANDY RAE

Planet Wolf - Wolves and War - Conflict and Courage - Homage and Honour - Dragons and Destiny - Valour and Victory - Ambition and Alavidha - Paws and Planets - Tales and Tails.
Dragon Wulf - Journey and Jeopardy - Gossamer and Grass - Flames and Freedom.
Flying Colours - Rascals and Renegades - Outlaws and Overlords - Sparkles and Sphinxes*.
T'Quel Magic - Ephemeral Boundary - Enduring Barrier - Eternal Bulwark.
Multiverse Muddle - Vampyre Crypt - Faie Castle - Surtr Chasm - Demon Citadel*.
Sammy the Cat - Cat in Charge - Cat at Christmas - Dog not in Charge.
Stand Alone - Kill by Cure.
(* Forthcoming as of Vampyre Crypt publication date)

PROLOGUE

Our planet is in danger.

Some dangers come from threats we can do little about, like volcanoes and earthquakes and asteroids.

Some dangers are internal, manufactured or caused by humankind, like nuclear accidents and pollution and wars.

What the majority of us do not know is that there are other dangers ... from elementals, wayward deities and kindred, and monsters ... there are always the monsters ... sometimes imagined ... sometimes real ... but always dangerous.

CANDY RAE

CHAPTER 1

THE PRESENT DAY

"Five tomahawks, wi blude red-rusted"

SOMEWHERE IN ENGLAND

Bumping along in the back of the container lorry, the prisoners had no idea where they were being taken but could guess it was nowhere good.

The five guards, one always standing watching them on a seat behind the driver's cabin, the others at the back beside the doors, were the scariest creatures they had seen outside of a horror film.

Oliver, who had been snatched from the street late the previous night was coming out of his drug 'high'.

The only nebulous memory of the abduction, and that memory was so vague it might as well have been a dream, was of a yellow vehicle coming to a stop at the kerb close to where he had been lying trying to get some sleep.

He couldn't remember being taken, being put into the container he was now inside, or being shackled to the metal sides by his wrists and ankles. They were hurting pretty bad now that he was awake.

To his left was an unconscious girl he knew as Phoebe. He had met her at the food bank canteen and had seen her around.

To his right was Ethan, a friend who was, like him, homeless and forced to live on the streets.

Oliver felt a bit better for a moment of two after recognising Ethan but the feeling quickly dissipated when he at last began to understand what must have happened.

They had been kidnapped!

He had got that far in his mental perambulations when he was violently sick, all down his front.

He heard unsteady footsteps approaching, unsteady because, as he realised, his metal-sided prison was moving.

Someone grabbed at Oliver's hair and pulled his head up. Oliver focused on his captor's head then wished he hadn't.

There was something about the face …

The eyes were black where they should have been white and white where they should have been coloured.

Who has eyes like that?

The iris was white.

What disease causes that?

The pupil was black, like the outside where it should have been white.

Oliver was groggily confused but aware that all was not well.

There was absolutely no way his captor was a member of the human race.

I should have paid more attention in biology classes at school. Teacher tried but I didn't listen.

The long, thin face was pale and the skin clammy, and there was no hair where the fuzz of a beard should have been, none at all.

Oliver's brain was beginning to start rationalising and he began to think about where he was and what was happening. *Definitely not human. So who? No! What is it? Some sort of vampire? Or a zombie?*

Oliver felt something cold and hard at his throat. Glancing down, he saw an axe.

Without any warning his head was pulled back. Pain exploded as the Kobold rammed it hard against the metal bars that ran along the container's side.

Oliver passed out.

One of the guards laughed and called out something in a language Simon didn't know to one of the other guards. He grinned, lifted the axe he was polishing and examined the sharpness of the edge.

YORKSHIRE - ENGLAND

Vin-ran-olt-hix woke with a start.

Someone was knocking at the door to his chamber.

His long fingered hand gripped his knife handle tighter. Vin-ran-olt-hix always took his rest with a minimum of three secreted about his person. One could never be too careful. His predecessor had died under an assassin's knife, his as a matter of fact.

However, it was very unlikely that an assassin would knock on his door to announce Vin-ran-olt-hix's imminent demise. He permitted his body to relax, a little bit.

"Who is it?" he called.

"Ahn-ran-hix, Your Worshipfulness."

What a crawler, thought Vin-ran-olt-hix, who wasn't over fond of his second-in-command but was stuck with him … for the time being. Ahn-ran-hix was a current favourite of Goddess Cailleach and it behoved him to tread carefully.

"Why have you disturbed my slumbers?" he asked in such a voice that a lowlier kobold than Ahn-ran-hix would probably have slunk away in fear for his life, however miserable that might be.

"San-hix has arrived with the prisoners."

"I will come," Vin-ran-olt-hix announced, fully awake and eager to find out what San-hix's group had managed to scoop up this time.

The prisoners were, in number twenty-seven, a goodly number. Vin-ran-olt-hix allowed San-hix his moment of glory as the Zapovjednik ushered the shackled, stumbling prisoners into the cavernous holding pen.

Some of those captured were young. If they were fed and watered properly, they might last a long time, especially if they weren't drained of too much blood at once.

Vin-ran-olt-hix smiled, his long canine teeth quivering with anticipation. He licked his lips. The thought of a pint of new drawn human blood was almost too much to bear.

He nodded to the Kobold who was in charge of the live food and pointed to the youngest female.

The Kobold understood.

Vin-ran-olt-hix wished to drink her blood direct from a vein and not extracted, strained and decanted into a sterilised bottle.

Phoebe shrank back as the Kobold headed straight for her, his snakelike tongue flicking in and out.

Simon shut his eyes but he couldn't block out the screams.

OSU INCIDENT ROOM 'ZULU ALPHA 5' - SCOTLAND

"Sir!"

The sergeant poked his head inside his superior's office. "Something's come in you might like to take a look at."

Interest piqued, Jamie Strachan had never brought him a report that was uninteresting, Inspector Finn MacMillan of Police Scotland's OSU looked up.

Jamie entered the room, carefully closing the door behind him.

"It's not on our patch, nor our remit," he began, "but …"

"But what?"

"What the report is saying looks familiar."

"To one of our cases?"

"One of our *peripheral* cases," answered Jamie.

Jamie was now in possession of *one hundred per cent* of Finn's interest. He didn't wait for the nod to proceed. The two had been working together for over three years and last year Jamie had been taken fully into Finn's confidence. Absolute trust and openness was implicit within that confidence.

"Remember that suspected explosion on the Isle of Rùm?"

"Aye. We were going to look into it, take a ferry from Mallaig but the ferries were off due to a storm. Didn't the Coastguards investigate?"

Jamie nodded. "They found nothing. Said it might have been a boat exploding but no wreckage was ever found. The people who originally reported it were returning from a party, rather inebriated if I recall. Report was signed off, naethin', nada, zilch. We were busy with that other matter up near Loch Assynt at the time."

"I remember *that* day. I've never seen so much rain. Soaking wet right through to my skin."

"That's the one sir."

"We didn't find anything there either," mused Finn.

"No," admitted Finn but he didn't sound absolutely convinced.

"You're thinking about those tracks we saw?"

"Aye. I am. I was positive than that there was something going on in the area and I still am. I said then those boot prints we found belonged to a couple of those nasty bloodsucking creatures whose base you've been trying to find since I came to the OSU. That's why I've brought you this."

He passed an evidence photograph over.

Finn's eyes opened as he looked at the footprint images captured by the crime scene investigators.

"I see what you mean," agreed Finn. "The outlines do look similar. Measurements?"

"Almost *exactly* the same."

"Where?"

Jamie checked his notebook.

"Outside the pigsties of a farm close to the hamlet of Thorgill, Ryedale, North York Moors National Park."

"Yorkshire again eh?"

"Nearest town is a place called Rosedale Abbey, eight or so miles south of Pickering."

Finn sat back in his chair, deep in thought.

"I don't think we need to go racing off into England," he said at last. "At least not until we get something more concrete."

"The farmer reported four pigs missing."

Finn laughed. It was blatantly obvious Jamie wanted to go and have a look.

"Still a no," he said with a grin.

"What about something about a dropped weapon? Would that help to change your mind? Reports say it's some type of axe."

"Now that's a little different but not so different that it would warrant a trip south. You're talking about that stash of axes those tourists found last year?"

"Yes. Those five tomahawks found outside the village of Beck Hole, also in the North York Moors National Park."

"That's the one. How far from Pickering was that?"

"About seventeen miles."

"Coincidence?"

Jamie grinned.

"You always tell me there's no such thing as a coincidence."

"You're right. I believe it's more than likely there's a connection. But I can't warrant the trip. Organise a report outlining our thoughts and what facts we have. Send it up to Daidh at the castle and a copy to Raibert at Finlarig House ... also make sure our people down there get a copy."

A disappointed Jamie left to do his bidding and Finn tried to settle back down to wading through a number of official matters in great need of his attention. He found it hard to concentrate, his thoughts lingering on large misshapen footprints and axes.

He had a gut feeling they hadn't heard the last about the North York Moors National Park.

YORKSHIRE - ENGLAND

Simon watched as the Kobold dragged the terrified, screaming, struggling Phoebe away, knowing his turn would come. He would leave the horror that was his prison. He would be taken to a place he did not know; to suffer a fate he didn't want to imagine.

Those who were taken away did not come back.

To his right was an empty space, the shackles dangling from the damp stone wall … where Ethan had been.

He had been taken away and had not come back.

CHAPTER 2

FIGHT IN THE HILLS

"Five scymitars, wi' murder crusted."

FINLARIG HOUSE - PERTHSHIRE - SCOTLAND

Ten days after the abduction of the twenty-seven and the day after the agonising death of Simon, a routine traffic report came in about a yellow minivan that had jumped a red light.

Raibert Mac Prainnseas Frisealach, or as he was known in the world that was not Faie, Robert MacFraser, had been keeping a weather eye out for a yellow minivan for a considerable time.

Although some believed he was on a hiding to nothing, Raibert, like Finn, did not believe in coincidences.

The mysterious minivan had been reported as a vehicle of interest in connection with some rather strange events that had taken place during the last few years.

Raibert had wanted 'to arrange a meeting' between one of his teams and the occupants of the minivan since the day his pointed ears had first twitched with interest.

He rang the away team members one at a time and uttered the same words.

"My place. Fourteen hundred hours."

OSU INCIDENT ROOM 'ZULU ALPHA 5' - SCOTLAND

"Sir! Message from Raibert's merry little band. They're going after that yellow minivan."

An eyes-wide-open-alert Inspector Finn MacMillan looked up.

"What yellow minivan?"

Jamie Strachan proceeded to tell him.

"Right," said Finn MacMillan, (or Fionn Mac na Maoile as he was known in the world that was Faie), once he had been reminded about the evidence they had about the van. "Give him as much help as we can, even if it means bringing in *our* people who are off duty and sending those who we don't want interfering on wild goose chases anywhere and anywhen, out of Raibert's way. If Raibert thinks the van is the one that belongs to the enemy then it is the van."

"Will do," grinned Jamie. He enjoyed these games of cat and mouse.

Faie recruits had begun to sign up for a police career not long after the end of the Second World War. Nowadays, there were around a hundred pureblood Faie, part-blood Daonna and Aonnan (all-human friends of the Faie) working within Police Scotland and double that number in Wales and England.

So although he had not yet received Jamie Strachan's report, Raibert had been aware of the increasing number of depredations amongst the homeless in the large cities over the border in England for some time.

A few years ago, there had been a spate of abductions in two of Scotland's cities, Glasgow and Stirling. The media had been convinced it was either a serial killer (perhaps a gang of serial killers) or perhaps a mobile group of human traffickers. The Faie knew better.

Raibert was in overall charge of the away teams responsible for hunting down and eradicating the perpetrators but he knew this might be his last time he commanded a team. He had received word last week that he was to hand over the reins to his second in command, one Concobhar MacGabhann and return to the castle where the king was waiting with a new assignment.

But first, there was the little matter of the yellow minivan.

The vehicle in question had been captured on CCTV footage four times during the last week, all in the same areas and at the same times as the recent abductions down in England. The van had then been sighted on the M1 heading north by one of Leicestershire Police's motorway patrols, a patrol manned by two Faie. Once sighted, each and every Faie, Daonna and Aonnan had been alerted and reports as to the location of the minivan, even after it exited the motorway, had started coming in fast and furious.

SOUTH WEST SCOTLAND

The occupants of the yellow minivan had no idea they had been clocked for what they were. They were travelling northwards in a light-hearted fashion, or at least in as light-hearted a fashion as the Kobold *could* exist. The Kobold, either as a race or individually were not renowned for a sense of humour.

Raibert's away team received another update.

The minivan had crossed the border into Scotland and was now travelling up the M74 towards Glasgow.

Everyone thought it would continue up through Scotland's largest city, on to the M80, then up the A9 to Perth.

It didn't. It took the exit on to the A71 and headed towards Ayrshire.

Raibert turned round in his seat to speak to Concobhar who was sitting in the back with another two warrior-kerns.

"That's a turn up for the books," he said. "I've never known them to move around in this area. They've always avoided the west coast south of Argyll and gone north."

"They must suspect we're on to them?" said Concobhar.

Raibert shook his head.

"I don't believe they do. They'd've used the minor roads in England if they had in an attempt to throw us off before they crossed the border. They know there are far more of us up here than down there."

"So where d'you think they're heading?"

"Your guess is as good as mine. Hrolfr! Andaer-Chi has his home down here somewhere. Give him a call. Phone number's on my mobile."

"Andaer-Chi?"

"My old tutor. Andaer Mac Aodghan Bruis. He's pretty ancient by now but he's in full possession of all of his marbles."

"Any relation to Andaerean Mac Andaer Bruis?" asked Concobhar, who knew the latter well.

"His father."

"Number's ringing," announced Hrolfr from the back.

The Faie were not the only protagonists in possession of a communications network. The Kobold had one as well, and they had

11

clocked the away team vehicles, consisting of a people carrier and a van, turning on to the A71.

They warned the yellow minivan and it began to drive faster.

The van passed through Strathaven at a fair lick and reached the little village of Drumclog where it turned off the main road and headed for the town of Muirkirk.

Unfortunately for them, Raibert's old tutor, Andaer lived close by and after Hrolfr's call had driven down to the main road and waited.

He alerted one of the local police cars. The Faie police officers waited for the minivan north of the town and when it passed, followed it.

The Kobold did not know these were not ordinary policemen and the driver elected to drive safely and at a speed under the limit so's not to draw attention.

The minivan remained in front of the police car, hoping it would turn off the road.

The two vehicles reached Cumnock then New Cumnock and it was there that the Kobold decided they were being followed and chose to make a break for it. After all, it was only one police car with two officers inside. They were, here in the minivan, in number, twelve … and they were armed. They took the single-track road to Craigdarroch.

But Raibert's team of warrior-kerns was closing in and although there was a network of roads and tracks in the area, these tracks did not lead anywhere.

The away team vehicles followed the minivan down the road that was little more than a track whilst the police car drew to one side of the tarmacadam road to ride interference.

"We'll get them right there," said Concobhar, pointing to a point on the map. "There's a loop in the track. One of us goes one way and the other the opposite. They'll be trapped between us."

"Agreed," said Raibert and Concobhar gave the order.

Behind Raibert and his driver were Concobhar and the two brothers Hrolfr and Kailen. The accompanying vehicle followed for a moment or two then turned off.

The three vehicles were now driving round the loop, and the yellow minivan was rapidly running out of options.

< Contact. Wait. Out. >

The radio message told Raibert that the others had sighted the minivan.

"Put your foot down," Raibert ordered his driver and Élair, a young

Faie whose first mission this was, did, the off-road careering up and down the humps and bumps in an attempt to get to the point where the yellow minivan had stopped before the fight started.

Raibert checked his pistol, an old fashioned Browning Hi-Power, made sure the magazines were in his pocket and that his knives were accessible.

They were so far from any habitations a muffle shouldn't be necessary; those very helpful goddess enabled illusions of 'no one here' and forgetfulness.

The vast majority of humankind wasn't aware that the Faie existed nor that a war was being fought between them and the forces of evil. Raibert intended to keep it that way.

Behind him in the back he could hear Concobhar, Hrolfr and Kailen getting ready. Raibert flexed his shoulders. He hated wearing flak jackets but the Kobold they were ambushing would almost certainly be armed with handguns if not with larger (and more lethal) weapons.

Some years back they had taken out one of the away teams with an anti-tank missile.

< Under fire. Enemy 12. >

Twelve against ten were good odds. Raibert could remember a time when an away team of ten had faced over thirty enemy warriors.

"Have you got their location?" he yelled into the back.

"Three minutes," Hrolfr yelled back, tightening his helmet strap.

The SUV's engine groaned as Élair put her foot down to the floor as she reached a straight bit of road. They couldn't spy what was happening ahead, because the trees were too high and thick. They went up a hill and as they careered over the top, they could at last see what was happening.

The away team's vehicle was burning, but the yellow minivan wasn't going anywhere either. It lay on its side.

"Shit," said Raibert under his breath. The Goddess only knew what had been happening but at least their compatriots had seen their approach.

< One Wounded. We're up the slope in the trees. Holding. >

"Stop here!" Raibert commanded and the SUV came to an abrupt halt. Raibert marvelled that he hadn't gone through the windscreen.

"We'll come at them from behind," he stated, after another quick examination of the detailed military map of the area.

They all had them on their tablets, a system ' borrowed' from a certain friendly, military source.

Raibert led them out, Élair bringing up the rear, everyone falling into a prone position when he reached a convenient rock. Whipping out his binoculars, he spied the other members of the team in cover beside some rocks on the east side of the track.

On the west side, in the ditch, were the Kobold, firing at the rocks. They did not appear to have seen the SUV.

"Don't see any lookouts," noted Concobhar, scanning the area on his own account.

"They never seem to bother," commented Raibert in a dry voice. "Must be some sort of failing in their make up."

Concobhar grinned, appreciating the joke.

"How many in the ditch?" asked Élair.

"I can count four, maybe five," said Kailen.

"Should be more than that," said Concobhar, pressing forward slightly the better to see.

"Watch out!" cried Kailen, who had spied movement up on a hillock, a glint of sun on glass, an instant, nothing more.

Concobhar's head hit the grass beside Élair.

Shocked, she looked over at the pool of blood forming under his head.

Raibert felt his pulse.

"He's gone. Hrolfr … did you see where that came from?"

The kern was already sighting his rifle, fiddling with the scope. He and his brother were excellent snipers.

Élair watched fascinated as Hrolfr's rifle moved slightly to the right.

"He's moving … three o'clock," said Kailen.

Hrolfr's finger squeezed the trigger and the movement at three o'clock stopped.

"Got him!" said Hrolfr, in satisfaction.

Élair was staring at Concobhar's lifeless body. It was the first dead warrior-kern she had seen.

"Let that be a lesson to you, young Élair," said Kailen. "Never expose yourself unless you know there's no one there."

"And even then … don't," added Hrolfr.

"He, he was just talking to me, in the SUV," stammered Élair but nobody answered, the brothers rolling off to the right as indeed what she had been taught to do when in battle lest the enemy homed in on your firing position, so, perforce, she followed. There would be time to mourn Concobhar later.

"He was always one to take risks," whispered Kailen to Hrolfr, who nodded.

Raibert followed them in short order, one never knew, the Kobold might have bigger weapons around ... and another sniper.

Once they had reached another location with rock cover, Raibert decided that the fight needed to be ended ... now ... before there was another Faie death.

He radioed the other half of the team.

< You get the rocket launcher out? >

The reply was in the affirmative.

< Fire the damn thing. >

Élair held her breath.

She heard a bang and the area where the Kobold were taking shelter disappeared in a cloud of smoke, fire and dust. There was no way of knowing how many, if any, had survived.

"Come on," shouted Kailen, getting to his feet. "Let's go!"

Élair didn't think she would ever forget that mad dash down the hill, weaving left and right to make her body as difficult a target as she could.

Not all the Kobold had died when the shell hit.

She hadn't realised until today what bullets sounded like as they whistled past an ear.

She also hadn't realised how the mixture of terror and adrenalin would feel.

She hit the deck just as the enemy fire began raining down.

A round hit her flak jacket and in that moment, Élair believed she was going to die.

But then, she heard the yelling voices of the other half of the away team as they charged the enemy.

Charged?

She could hardly believe her eyes. They were actually running towards the Kobold!

"Come on!" yelled Kailen in her ear as he dragged her upright and forward. "They've dropped their guns!"

The fighting was hand-to-hand now.

There were Kobold still alive in what was the horror of the impact crater, all wielding those curved swords they were so fond of. She remembered the lessons of Zellair-Chi in the salle over the years. Kobold would do everything in their power not to be taken alive. They also preferred to die with a blade in their hand, fighting and hopefully bringing down the enemy before they took a last breath.

Pulling sword from sheath, Élair joined the mêlée.

CANDY RAE

CHAPTER 3

KING'S CHOICE

"While we sit bousing at the nappy,
And getting fou and unco happy."

CAISTEAL NA SÌOBHRAGAN - SCOTLAND

"Concobhar's body is being returned to his family," said Aed Mael, discerning his friend's thoughts.

Raibert and the High King were walking along the battlements, deep in thought.

The High King was thinking about the options before him and Raibert *had* been thinking about his fallen comrade.

"It puts a problem in our way. As you know, I was going to give Concobhar-Chi command of the away teams."

Raibert nodded. "And now you don't know what to do for the best? I could stay with the team."

Aed Mael shook his head.

"That's not the solution. The Army needs a commanding officer. You are the best choice. Your appointment as Ceannard stands."

"You could bring Kiah back to lead the teams."

"I could, or I could give command to Nansaidh-Chi."

Raibert shook is head.

"She's my choice as my second-in-command. What about bringing Andaerean-Chi back from England?"

Aed Mael shook his head again.

"What he's doing down there is too important. No. You and Nansaidh will have to command both the away teams and the army for the time being. Find someone able to take command."

Raibert thought about what this would entail for a moment before commenting.

"We'll manage for a while but perhaps it's time for Fionn-Chi to leave the police and come and join us full time."

"Perhaps it is," Aed Mael. I'll think about it … meanwhile … I've got a decanter of fine brandy in my snug and a geòidh leann only half empty. Care to join me? We could talk about old times and get drunk."

Raibert smiled. He liked brandy but *loved* the taste of heather honey beer.

"And to remember Concobhar. He was a good friend and a good Faie but he never could remember to keep his head down in a fight."

OSU INCIDENT ROOM 'ZULU ALPHA 5' - SCOTLAND

"Vicious little fight they had down by Cumnock," said Jamie Strachan to Finn MacMillan. "Two of ours dead. And …" he paused impressively, "instead of axes the team collected five scimitars. I wonder if that's important … the number five I mean."

For once, Finn wasn't paying his subordinate much attention, his eyes riveted on the signal flimsy in his hand.

"What's that?" he asked.

Jamie reiterated his comments, this time with half of his superior's attention.

"Yes."

Jamie gave up and left to get on with other matters.

Finn read the words again.

He didn't know whether to be pleased or happy with the news that he was to take charge of the away teams.

He was pleased because he would become closer to his kindred, the Faie … but he would miss his life in the police.

Fionn-Chi sighed.

He would start the resignation ball rolling in the morning but he knew it would take some time for his superiors to arrange for the arrival of his replacement.

He picked up the other message, an invite to Raibert's Finlarig House for the weekend following. He started cancelling his other engagements.

CHAPTER 4

DREAMS OF THE GODDESS

*"For auld lang syne, my jo, for auld lang syne,
We'll tak' a cup o' kindness yet, for auld lang syne."*

SOMEWHERE IN THE MULTIVERSE

Goddess Flidais was in a quandary.

It was forbidden to interfere directly in the affairs of her world so how was she going to get her messages across to the Faie?

I'll have to go back to what I did before, she decided, and hopefully they'll get the significance of the link between the words and the place. It's a pity the words aren't completely the same as the place but that can't be helped. My Faie aren't complete idiots!

Once that was decided, Goddess Flidais went through the various versions of the poem and decided what lines to use.

She was having difficulty deciding between two of them.

So do I use 'For auld lang syne, my jo, for auld lang syne; We'll tak' a cup o' kindness yet, for auld lang syne'? Or do I use 'On old long syne, my Jo, on old long syne; That thou canst never once reflect on old long syne'? Or do I use a lot more quotes, or will that muddy the waters too much?

After some thought, she decided that too much was better than too little. When word got out about the dreams, the enemy would be sure to learn of it and a little muddying might go a long way to keep them from finding out what was happening.

The Faie who were the most likely to comprehend the significance of the words were certain to make the connection.

That problem solved, Flidais began thinking about other ways she could help without contravening her father's rules.

Flidais had forgotten the mortal brain's capacity to remember and the fact that her message-dreams had in the past, only got through to the children.

CHAPTER 5

CHILD OF THE FAIE

"The lightnings flash from pole to pole;
Near and more near the thunders roll."

PERTHSHIRE - SCOTLAND

It was a stormy night, so stormy that Aksel-Chi was wondering if the chimney pots would blow off the house opposite!

It was so exciting to know that he was going off to school at last.

Aksel liked his friends well enough but it would be nice not to have to hold his tongue about what he was and where he had come from.

He lived with his family, (his parents, and two much younger sisters) on a small dairy farm. He had been attending the small, local, primary school in a village up the road but now that he was ten it was time to say goodbye to his little playmates and move on to a senior school. In fact, there were two and neither were at all like the schools his friends and the majority of schoolchildren out in the world would have recognised. They were where the Faie went to learn specific skills as well as more usual subjects like maths and languages and sciences.

The first boarding school facility was at Caisteal Na Sìobhragan, the huge castle that was the seat of the king and the centre of his governance in Scotland.

The second was at Sith Talla. From the outside, it looked, when all was said and done, rather like a number of interconnecting prison buildings surrounded by a high wall. However, it had not been built to keep prisoners in but to keep enemies out in order to protect the precious students inside.

As at the castle, there were dormitories for the youngsters and individual bedrooms for the older students, classrooms, lecture halls, recreation areas and a kitchen and dining facility, the same as any other boarding facility. But what they might not have, Sith Talla did, possessing no less than two salles (indoor halls for learning how to use weapons), an underground shooting range and a number of guardrooms.

Aksel, although he might have wished it could be so, would not spend all of his time at Sith Talla.

He would spend a good half of each term at Caisteal Na Sìobhragan where he would attend academic classes. He might even take external exams like the students attending non-Faie schools. One entire area of the huge castle complex was dedicated to education and research.

He was worried however that he might be behind those who had attended one of the two Faie junior schools or had been taught by a tutor.

He was ready for the big adventure.

His trunk was packed.

His weapons carrier was packed, the sword his father had carried at his age carefully set inside the padded box together with his bow, knives and revolver, for Aksel's training would include how to use them all.

He went to bed that last night trying to suppress his excitement, wondering if he would be able to get any sleep at all, especially with the storm winds howling in the rafters, hoping the bad weather wasn't an omen.

He settled down to sleep eventually, but only after his mother threatened that if he didn't he wouldn't go to the castle in the morning.

He lay awake in silence for some time, listening to the wind and tracing the patterns on the wall panels, but at last his eyes began to flicker shut.

His breathing deepened.

Askel was asleep.

His dream was accompanied by a woman's voice … singing.

"Should auld acquaintance be forgot, and never brought to mind?
Should auld acquaintance be forgot, and auld lang syne?
For auld lang syne, my jo, for auld lang syne,
We'll tak' a cup o' kindness yet, for auld lang syne."

CHAPTER 6

SWORDS CAN KILL

"Prime, Seconde, Tierce, Quarte, Quinte, Sixte, Seprime, Octave, Neuvieme."

SITH TALLA - SCOTLAND

Aksel was right in the middle of yet another restless, interrupted night.

It was that voice again, that woman's voice, singing the lines. *'On old long syne my Jo, on old long syne.'*

He banged his head on the pillow in an attempt to stop it and it did go away. However, what replaced it was almost worst. It was Weaponsmaster Zellair's voice counting out the sword parrying positions and if it wasn't his voice saying variations of *Prime, Seconde, Tierce, Quarte, Quinte, Sixte, Seprime, Octave, Neuvieme*, it was his voice explaining the picture of a person's torso with the same words but in a different order. Why did *Tierce* go with *Sixte* and why were they together?

It was all very confusing.

Aksel had been a pupil at Sith Talla and Caisteal Na Sìobhragan for two months now and was enjoying life up to the hilt.

He had made friends and much to his relief he had found he wasn't behind anyone else educationally, that is in the '3R's' (reading-riting-rithmetic). Only about a third of those in his classes had attended one of the two small junior schools in the country run by the Faie, or had been taught be a governess or governor. The only subjects the two thirds needed to catch up with were Faie specific areas in history, geography and language ... and weapons training. A number of the new students were advanced for their age and others less so.

Aksel and those compeers who were aged between ten and thirteen had begun their studies at the castle, taking tests to assess their standard and what classes they would need to attend. They had then gone to Sith Talla to begin their practical classes.

Aksel wrote to his father thanking him for taking the time to show him some basic moves in knife fighting. He was also now appreciating the fact that his parents had made him join an archery club back home. Here he had won all but one of the shooting competitions the archery instructors would set up for his year group and now attended archery class with some older pupils.

As the ten-year-old Askel was a member of the class made up of ten to thirteen year olds, he found himself behind the older class members in sword and knife fighting, especially those who had been here for a number of years.

He didn't like this and had vowed to catch up as soon as he could.

Fechtmesiter (Weaponsmaster) Zellair was in charge of, in his own words, 'trying to teach them enough so that they don't get killed'. His speciality was fighting with blades.

Askel asked one of his friends, a girl two years older than him, why they spent so much time learning to fight with swords and knives.

His shoulders ached at the end of each and every one of his sword classes and if anyone had asked his opinion (which they had not) he would have told them that he would like to specialise in one of the less strenuous disciplines.

"What's wrong with guns and bullets?" he asked Sineag-Chi.

Sineag explained that although in this world the High God Jah had permitted the use of ballistic weapons, that on the other worlds this was not the case.

"The Holocene is the first world Jah has allowed it," she told Aksel.

"Why?"

"Because on the other worlds there hasn't been an industrial revolution like there has here," she explained. Sineag liked explaining things.

"I don't understand."

"It wouldn't be fair to use guns and things where they haven't been invented yet," she answered, somewhat evasively.

Aksel sort of accepted her explanation and resolved to get an answer from an adult.

However, apart from the occasional difficulty, Aksel was enjoying learning how to use weapons. It was certainly better than mathematics class.

Today they had been told they were going to learn all about falling.

Aksel couldn't understand what falling had got to do with swords and lunges and parries but he had been learning quite a few queer things lately so he didn't really question the topic.

If Zellair-Chi wanted him to learn how to fall, then learn how to fall he would.

As the class made its usual noisy entrance into the salle, they were brought up short and fell silent.

Zellair was not the only instructor standing inside the door.

With him were no less than three very important people, Àrd-Righ Aed Mac Searc Gwrtheyrn Mael, the King; Ceannard Raibert Mac Prainnseas Frisealach, Commander of the Army; and Fo Ceannard Nansaidh Nic Ellair Druimeineach, Raibert's second-in-command.

Askel didn't know whether to salute, bow or run away!

"Come in, come in. Gather round," called Zellair and once the unusually silent class were standing in front of him, he explained that although they would be studying unarmed combat and falling during the second part of the practice time, the first half hour or so would be spent watching the four adults giving a demonstration of swordplay, including how a planned and practiced fall could get a fighter out of some deadly situations.

The class found places on the benches at the end of the salle and prepared to be amazed. Sineag whispered to Aksel that they were in for a treat and so it proved.

The four performed a demonstration of techniques in slow time and in real time.

Aksel was amazed at the speed and dumfounded about how they managed to react to the attacking moves of the others in a split second.

He decided then and there that he was going to practice and practice until he was as good.

He was also thunderstruck when he saw how fit and supple they all were and how they used that suppleness to squirm out of trouble. No less a person than the king feinted a fall so as to put his opponent for the moment, it was Nansaidh, at a disadvantage when everyone thought she had the advantage.

Eventually, Zellair called a halt and the four stopped. Not one was puffing and panting.

Aed Mael grinned. He appeared to have been enjoying himself.

"Swords and agility work together," said Zellair. "A sword can kill, but it's what you do with a sword in your hand that can make the kill better, and perhaps save your life one day. When I was your age I sat where you are now and watched a similar demonstration.

My father was one of the four and he gave us a lecture, a rather boring lecture if I recall so I am not going to repeat it. I'm going to say what I want to say in two sentences."

There were a number of relieved sighs from his audience.

"Swords are hand held killing machines. They are dangerous, so be careful, especially during this time of learning … unless of course an army of Kobold appears and attacks us."

There were grins and titters of laughter from the audience.

With that admonition Aed Mael left them.

Nansaidh and Raibert left the salle a short time later, leaving Zellair to take the rest of the lesson.

Nansaidh laughed.

"That reminded me of that time when we were not much older than them and were yawning through that speech of Àrd-Righ Searc Mael. Didn't you fall asleep?"

"I might have done," admitted Raibert.

"Who was there? Me, you and Caoimhe, Daidh and Aed Mael of course. But there was someone else …"

"Nimue," said Raibert. "She'd come up for a visit."

"That's right. She was Caoimhe's friend. How did they know each other?"

"There were four of us under Nanny's command in the nursery at Finlarig," answered Raibert, closing his eyes as memories threatened to overwhelm him. "Aed Mael, Caoimhe, Nimue and me."

CHAPTER 7

INTO THE PAST

FOUR FRIENDS

"Sing a Song of Sixpence"

FINLARIG HOUSE - PERTHSHIRE - SCOTLAND

Nanny always sang it at bedtime.

> *"Sing a Song of Sixpence,*
> *A bag full of Rye,*
> *Four and twenty Naughty Boys,*
> *Baked in a Pye."*

When Raibert was old enough to ask why she sang it he was told it was a reminder to be good. Once Raibert was old enough to ask some deeper questions, Nanny's answer changed.

"But your words are different from the ones we sing at school," he said. "We sing …

> *"Sing a song of sixpence,*
> *"A pocket full of rye,*
> *"Four and twenty blackbirds*
> *"Baked in a pie."*

"That is because I am very old," Nanny Ceiteig answered. "The one I sing comes from a book I was given when I was not much older than you."

"How old is very old?"

"I am a hundred and fifty years old," smiled Nanny.

"That's old," marvelled Raibert. "John's granny at school, she's seventy-five, a whole lot less than you and he says she's *very* old. And I've seen a photo and she's all grey and wrinkly and you don't. Why do you look so much younger?"

"Have you been talking about your home and family to your friends?"

"Well, just a little bit."

"Raibert! What is the rule?"

"Not to speak of home."

"Why?"

"Because we are different than them."

That was the end of school for the young Raibert Mac Prainnseas Frisealach, alias Robert MacFraser, or if he were given the pure Faie honorific, Raibert-Chi.

The very next week the tutor arrived, together with three live-in school friends.

Raibert's father was a very important person. Although Faie, he worked in the human world, being a Procurator Fiscal based in Inverness, over five hours train-ride away. He wasn't home much, what with his day job and his duties to the World of the Faie. His mother had died when he was a baby so Nanny was his only companion, at least until the others arrived. She had looked after his mother and his mother's mother and for all Raibert knew, his mother's mother's mother too.

His father had another avocation, as a warrior-kern in King Searc Mael's army, charged with fighting to defend the land, not against other peoples but against the minions of the Goddess Cailleach, in a war that had lasted eons.

Raibert's father liked to think that he was an upholder of law, peace and order in two worlds, the 'seen' and the 'unseen', the human and the non-human.

Finlarig House, the family home, was old, but not so old as Nanny, having been built in the early nineteenth century of stout stone with a robust wall around, and a moat. The house was also of the 'seen' and 'unseen' variety. Nanny told Raibert that the moat was very important because it helped keep the 'gyres' away. He knew that there was an illusion round his home because his little friends at the nursery called his house a cottage and Raibert knew fine well that it was too big to be a cottage like the other farm cottages around.

Raibert knew all about the 'gyres' and illusions because he was of the Faie.

The Faie were one of the kindred collectively known as the Cuetiachtli or the Children of the Gods. There were six kindred, the Druas, the Sidhe, the Siofra, the Fladhaich, the Ljosalfar, and the Faie but only the latter were here on this planet, in this part of the multiverse, in the here and now.

There were two other races able to survive in Scotland and in other parts of the world, the Kobold and the Spriggan. They were the followers of the Goddess Cailleach and her brother, the God Balar, the sworn enemies of the Goddess Flidais and her Faie.

For a Faie child, growing up took the same number of years as a human child. It was after about twenty years that everything slowed down. If a Faie didn't die by an unnatural cause, they might expect to live about a hundred and eighty years. They aged slower. A forty-year-old Faie would look almost the same as they did at twenty.

The nursery four were all about the same age.

First to arrive was one of the younger sons of King Searc Mael, Prince Aed. Aed-Chi.

Second to arrive was Nimue-Chi, the daughter of a prominent Faie from the Stewartry of Kirkcudbright.

Last to arrive was a young Faie from Ireland, one Caoimhe-Chi. She was an orphan, her parents having died in a fight against some Kobold the previous year.

Nanny opened her heart and gathered them in, giving them the love and security they craved, especially Aed and Caoimhe. As the younger son of the king, Aed felt he was not valued and was ignored because he was not destined for kingship and Caoimhe had been shunted from pillar to post since the deaths of her parents.

Raibert was a generous child and didn't mind the attention Nanny gave to the others, at least not very much.

Nimue wasn't interested in attention. She was a very self-sufficient young lady and clever with it. Although the youngest, she could read and write better than the other three and she was much better at figuring.

Raibert and the others thought this very unfair but weren't unkind to the prodigy (Aed had heard Nanny calling her by this name - it sounded very important).

Nimue loved poetry, especially the old kind, the sagas and poems of bygone ages, Faie and Human.

She told the other three that when she grew up she was going to become a learned professor, or a translator or perhaps a famous author.

Raibert thought she might just do all three, although Aed was inclined to ridicule the idea.

"You think you're another Bettisia Gozzadini?" he mocked.

"Who's she?" asked Caoimhe and Raibert.

But Aed knew little more than the name and that she had been the first, in his words, of the 'she people to teach at a university'.

As Caoimhe, Nimue and Raibert didn't know what a university was at this point in their lives, they weren't any the wiser.

However, they became a lot wiser about many other things after the arrival of their tutor.

He was called Andaer-Chi and was, according to Raibert, a much better teacher than the ones in the village school. He catered to their abilities and did his best not to be condescending when there were things they didn't understand.

The more 'normal' lessons, like the ones in the mainstream schools in the outside world he taught capably and well. The others he taught too, except for learning how to fight, although he oversaw their practice. A Weaponsmaster arrived once a week and spend the best part of the day training Andaer's young charges in the niceties of fighting with sword, knife and bow. Caoimhe was convinced he used magic to travel because when they went to bed he wasn't there and at breakfast he was, but she was from a part of Ireland where legends of magic were a part of life. Firearms training would come when they were older although they were taught how to make such weapons safe.

Raibert liked learning how to use weapons best of all. He had decided to be a warrior-kern when he grew up.

Aed liked this too but was more interested in rocks, especially when he got hold of a simplified report on a pre war article by an Alfred Wegener concerning continental drift. He had decided that duties permitting, he was a prince and knew he would have many duties when he grew up, he would like to be a scientist and if not that, a teacher.

Nimue continued to wish a future as a famous academic out in the world of the humans.

Caoimhe was a happy-go-lucky little girl who hadn't a clue what she wanted to be when she grew up and didn't care that she didn't.

The four were taught about the constant battle against the rebel Goddess Cailleach. They all knew something about it, Caoimhe more than most because her parents had died fighting the Kobold.

They were aware, from this young age, that the world was a dangerous place.

One morning the younglings woke to find that Andaer-Chi had been called away. Nanny informed them that she would be taking the morning lessons.

The careful operation of balancing the full spoon between the milk bowl and the porridge bowl came undone as Nimue's clattered on to the spotless scrubbed table.

Nanny tut-tutted. She was very good at the tut-tutting. She demanded that Nimue should be more careful as the nursery maid mopped up the spill.

As the meal progressed, the four snuck uncomfortable glances at each other. Nanny! What did she know about their lessons? She was Nanny for goddess sake!

But Nanny proved to be very good at spelling, reading and figuring. She did however, balk at the thought of elementary science. Science hadn't been on the curriculum when she had been a lass and she said as such.

"What do you want to do *instead*?" she asked, with a lot of emphasis on the last word. Fact was, Nanny was scared of most things scientific and she didn't want them to know about this being a chink in her formidable armour.

"We could do history?" suggested Caoimhe. She liked stories about the olden days.

"No. Literature," Nimue said, a hint of command in her voice.

"What about you two?" Nanny asked the two boys.

They had been edging along their seats (the schoolroom consisted of three two-seater bench desks with ink pots in the centre of the desk part).

"We were thinking of going to so some practice," said Raibert, "if you're finished with us that is."

"No. Andaer-Chi told me you were to lesson until noon ... but ... we could do some history and literature together if you like? I could tell you a story."

That stopped the boys and they slipped back to their places. Nanny was a champion storyteller.

"About when you were a little girl?" asked Caoimhe.

"Nanny. What was it like then?" asked Raibert, the most experienced in getting Nanny to talk.

Nanny loved to tell tales about her days when she had been not much older than they were now but she was not going to be fooled into telling them something not to do with their lessons.

"I'll tell you about my first job," she said.

"And the literature part?" pressed Nimue.

"We had poetry then too," said Nanny and began …

CHAPTER 8

NANNY'S TALE

"Little Robin Red breast."

FINLARIG HOUSE - PERTHSHIRE - SCOTLAND

"In the Year of Their Lord, Seventeen Hundred and Ninety, I worked in the nursery of the big house near Auldgirth," Nanny began.

"*The* Nanny?" asked Nimue.

"Not then. That came later," answered Nanny. "I was very young. *That* Nanny was an old woman, a human and she was old. She died a long time ago."

"We live a lot longer than humans," Nimue mentioned in passing but with a certain amount of satisfaction.

"It's not very nice to crow about it," chided Caoimhe in her lilting voice. "It's not their fault."

"Quite right," approved Nanny. "So there I was …"

"Was your family's house nearby?" Nimue interrupted.

"Yes. My family had lived there since the time when Scotland was not one country but many … but I thought you wanted to hear about me."

"Yes Nanny. Please go on," pleaded Aed, donating on Nimue a sour look.

"Most of my work wasn't directly with the children," said Nanny. "But one day every second week Nanny Riddel had a day out and off she would go and I would be looking after the bairns. I would sing them nursery rhymes, there was an old book and we would say them aloud and put airs to them. It was good fun."

"Sing us them … please!" Caoimhe pleaded.

"I can't remember them dearie, it was so long ago."

Caoimhe looked so disappointed that Nanny racked her brains and managed to *remember two. She sang the one she liked best first.*

"Little Robin Red breast,
Sitting on a pole,
Nidde, Noddle, Went his head.
And poop went his Hole."

Caoimhe gave an embarrassed little giggle while Aed and Raibert laughed.

"That's rude," declared Nimue, trying to look stern but Raibert realised she was interested, despite herself. Nimue always liked new things.

"Sing us another," begged Caoimhe.

After some thinking about what tune to set the next one to, Nanny complied.

"Ride a cock-horse
To Banbury Cross,
To see what Tommy can buy;
A penny white loaf,
A penny white cake,
And a two-penny apple-pie."

"An apple pie costing two pennies!" marvelled Aed. Aed loved apples.

"Perhaps they were bigger in the olden days," suggested Caoimhe.

"We could put our own tunes to them," declared Nimue, eager to show off her musical skills.

"So what else did you do?" asked Raibert in a hurry. Nimue's 'musical' demonstrations were to be avoided at all cost.

"Well … when I had my day off I would get up early and walk home to see my parents on their farm. On the way I would pass by another farm known as Ellisland and on the farm lived a family called Burns. It was Robert Burns the poet."

"Really! Really and truly?" gushed Nimue, closing in on Nanny. Not those silly nursery rhymes, but poetry, real poetry! How wonderful!

Raibert could see that Nanny's story would be a lengthy one now that Nimue had clocked on to one of Scotland's national bards. He had heard her recite bits from Tam O'Shanter.

As if she had read his mind, Nimue's voice piped up. "Were you there when he wrote Tam O'Shanter?"

"Yes I was. Do you want to hear a story about it?"

"Yes please."

Aed and Raibert prepared to be bored although Caoimhe settled down beside Nimue.

"It was part true," said Nanny. "The history books call it a legend but …"

"You know better," breathed Nimue.

"I was friends with one of their farm servants," said Nanny. "I used to visit. She had come up frae Ayrshire with the cows and didn't have many friends. And I met the bard, he was a good lookin' man. He had an eye for a bonnie lass; and I was a bonnie lass if I say so myself. We got to talking one day and I told him about the Faie legend of the Chase at Alloway Kirk except I missed out the word Faie."

"Tam O'Shanter," breathed Nimue.

Nanny smiled. "The Aonnan think the auld kirk is haunted, only we Faie really know why they think that."

"It'll be the Kobold," said Raibert, nodding his head like a little old wise man.

Nanny nodded and explained that the witches in Burn's poem were indeed Kobold and that the devil playing the bagpipes was the Goddess Cailleach herself. She also let slip that the farmer in the legend and the poem was actually her grandfather.

"He knew that water doesn't stop the Kobold and that was a bit of, bit of …"

"Poetic licence," said Nimue.

"Playing with the facts," said Raibert.

"The rest of it is pretty much as it happened," she added after finishing the story about how her grandfather fled over the river with the Kobold at his heels. "His horse didn't lose her tail neither, and grandfather, he wasn't drunk at all, he was returning from a tryst with my grandmother and she was a great hater of the smell of the whisky on the breath. Now the lot of you! Put your warm clothes on and get outside for some fresh air."

Nimue sighed; she had wanted to read the poem again in the light of what she had learned but knew there was no arguing with Nanny.

Later though, after tea, a wholesome tea of soft boiled dippy eggs and strips of toast, Nimue did read the poem again. She decided poetry was much more interesting if you knew the story behind it. Turning the page, she came across another Burns poem, *Auld Lang Syne*, and wondered about that one.

I must ask Nanny in the morning, she thought as she closed the book and laid it neatly on the table.

The Tam O'Shanter episode did have a consequence, as well as a reinforcement of Nimue's desire to become a literature professor.

Aed and Raibert formed a secret society they called 'Chase'. It wasn't a form of 'Catch me if you can' but a convoluted game about warriors fighting the baddies by going on missions and finding out things to help with the war against Cailleach.

The two boys soon got bored with it but Nimue embraced it with something akin to an addiction. She was always writing stories to do with them going on dangerous missions and coming back with all the answers.

"Like the quests in the Viking sagas," she told the other three. "And I've made up passwords and codes. When I'm an important person and I've got to tell you something really important I'll use the code ... one that only you three will understand."

But Aed and Raibert weren't interested in codes.

"The passwords will be really important one day," she told them.

Aed and Raibert weren't interested in passwords either.

"The heroes and heroines will need codes and passwords in the future," she insisted.

Aed and Raibert weren't at that stage in their lives when they were all that interested in their future, nor of being a hero. When Nimue told them heroic stories from the sagas they had noticed that the heroes usually died.

Caoimhe was more tolerant of Nimue's stories and fantastic plans for the future. She listened although she didn't always remember.

She did remember Nimue saying it was funny how letters of *Auld Lang Syne* had, hidden inside the words, the name of her family's manor house.

In time, the quartet was broken up.

Nimue went home to Kirkcudbrightshire. She was going to a boarding school in Edinburgh where she was to prepare for the university entrance exams.

Aed's eldest brother Eanruig was away fighting in Russia so he was called home to Caisteal Na Sìobhragan to help his father.

Raibert and Caoimhe remained at Finlarig House until they followed

Aed to the castle to complete their education.

When, many years later, Caoimhe married Raibert, she told him about Nimue and the name hidden in the words of *Auld Lang Syne* but he was so busy learning how to be a warrior, he forgot.

CHAPTER 9

VAMPYRE CRYPT

"The wind blew as 'twad blawn its last;
The rattling showers rose on the blast."

ROSEDALE ABBEY - YORKSHIRE - ENGLAND

While Nanny's quartet was playing in the Perthshire countryside, four were having a progress meeting, making plans and hatching plots.

"Now that the Aonnan are concentrating on this war in France, it is a good time to take back the initiative," said Zapovjednik Vin-ran-olt-hix, Goddess Cailleach's Commander-in-Chief. "We haven't been able to make much inroad into their territories. This is our chance."

The three other, more junior, zapovjedniks nodded gravely.

"San-hix," barked Vin-ran-olt-hix. "What have you to tell me about your failure at Fladhaich Dùn? Watch what you say, for our Goddess is, shall we say, a little peeved with you and she might be listening."

San-hix shook his pale, cavernous head. "It was not my fault," he whined. "The Guem were there in great numbers and the Ljosalfar too. They must have known we were coming."

"And how can that be?"

"I do not know, Your Worshipfulness."

"Leave your praying for our Goddess."

San-hix's face took on a despairing look as Vin-ran-olt-hix turned to look at the next Kobold.

Zen-hix cringed.

"What have you to tell me about your failure at Finla?" asked Vin-ran-olt-hix.

"It was not my fault," he whinged. "The Bloden were there in great numbers and the Fladhaich too. They have to have known we were coming."

"Both your excuses are remarkable in the fact they are the same. You might have thought to deflect Cailleach's anger but all you have done is to make it worse. I know her mind better than anyone alive. Will you accept my punishment or do you wish to plead?"

Incapable of speech, San-hix and Zen-hix lowered their eyes and pointed to Vin-ran-olt-hix. They knew that however bad Vin-ran-olt-hix's punishment; that of Cailleach would be a thousand times worse.

"Good. I'm glad you both understand the realities of the situation. Take off your helmets and drop your weapons."

There were two clangs as two swords and two chimes as two knives hit the stone floor of the crypt. A third chime signified the release of a wrist knife.

"Now the other."

A sixth weapon dropped. It tinkled as it hit the floor.

Vin-ran-olt-hix turned to face the third Kobold.

"Arrange for guards to take these two to the small dungeon then return. I will deal with them before supper."

Bin-hix bowed and turned to do his superior's bidding while at the same time trying to hide his smile of satisfaction.

He had done well on *his* mission, seeking out and killing no less than twenty-four Daonna who had been on the wanted list. The target had been eighteen so he was on a high of elation.

Vin-ran-olt-hix waited in silence until Bin-hix, accompanied by the guards, returned and waited, again in silence while the two condemned Kobold were taken away. He would enjoy killing these two. They hadn't realised he had known of their plot to overthrow him for some time and had planned their demise with a meticulousness born of a better cause. He would have been very surprised if they *had* completed their missions successfully.

Vin-ran-olt-hix hadn't been Cailleach's most trusted underling for so long without learning a few things.

Yes, he would enjoy watching their deaths and enjoy even more the taste of their blood.

He turned his gaze to Bin-hix. Could he trust him? Probably not, but for the time being, he would act as if he did.

He smiled at Bin-hix, displaying as he did his blood stained canine teeth.

Bin-hix met his gaze without flinching.

Vin-ran-olt-hix admired bravery amongst his Kobold, so long as it wasn't directed against him personally, or against his beloved goddess.

"So what can we do?" he asked.

"I have agents tracking all the sons and daughters of Searc Mael," Bin-hix informed him. "The Ri-Beag Eanruig is with his father at Caisteal Na Sìobhragan recovering from wounds incurred at Foinaven Mountain where, if you remember …"

"I do. Please continue."

"Word is that the Ri-Beag will recover and is heading for Russia in the near future. My agents intercepted a message. Prionnsa Torean is fighting with the soldiers in France. We have hopes of getting to him there."

"And the other son?"

"Nothing yet. We do know he was sent away to complete his education but we have not, as yet, been able to locate the place. It might be in Ireland, or elsewhere, perhaps Wyoming in America. It is, quite possibly, and might say probably, here in England. Agents are checking."

"The two females?"

"Both at Caisteal Na Sìobhragan although there are rumours of a marriage between the eldest, Bana-phrionnsa Elsbeth and one of their kind in Russia. That is, we believe one of the reasons for the Ri-Beag's visit there. The youngest is very young. There is no way we can assassinate them while they are at the castle."

"Concentrate on the males," ordered Vin-ran-olt-hix. "Ambush Eanruig when he recovers from his wounds. Kill the one in France. Make it look like an accident. That shouldn't be difficult. A nice little bomb crater in the trenches should dispose of any evidence. And find the young one. Cailleach has ordered them all dead. Now, I must go, I have two executions to oversee."

He licked his lips and Bin-hix shivered. He spared a thought for his two, soon to be late, comrades. It might be him one day.

Vin-ran-olt-hix saw the shiver and mentally laughed.

As he walked away he was thinking, keep that thought in mind young Bin-hix. If you do you might be able to live your full span of years. Or perhaps not. Ambition, while it gets things done, can be dangerous.

Above the crypt, in the rain and in the fresh air, two lovers were exploring the priory ruins.

It had been a Cistercian Priory, founded during the reign of King

Henry the Second of England by one William de Rosedale in 1158. There the Cistercian nuns had lived and worshipped there until King Henry the Eighth of England dissolved the monasteries in 1535, the nun's main claim to fame in the history books being a warning not to bring their lap-dogs into the church when celebrating the canonical hours because the dogs were distracting the nuns from their religious observances.

The only original parts of the priory above ground still standing, this after the Victorians had built a new church over the imprint of the priory church, were the remains of a turret staircase, a stone pillar and a sundial.

Underground was the hidden crypt that was the Kobold base.

They had other little hidden capsules situated throughout England, but the crypt was the largest. It was in the crypt that they fine-tuned their plans, punished those who failed to carry them out and worshipped Goddess Cailleach.

Above ground, the young woman and the young man, he was in army uniform and on embarkation leave prior to being sent to a place called Gallipoli in the Dardanelles, were looking for a place to be alone.

"There must be somewhere we can go that's out of the wind and rain," the young woman said with a giggle and a flirtatious look at the bushes beside the staircase. "It's rattling something awful. Hurry up, I go on shift in an hour."

"And my train leaves in three," he laughed as he followed her into the bushes.

It was presumed, when the young woman didn't turn up for her shift at the roasting kilns and the young man didn't report back to barracks; that they had run off together, perhaps to Ireland or even to the Americas. The young woman was declared missing and the young man absent without leave.

Neither was close to the truth. Indeed, none of those in charge of keeping records, whether in the police or in the military, would have believed the truth was true.

They would have said …

Vampyres?

Don't be ridiculous!

Vin-ran-olt-hix preferred the taste of Aonnan blood to Kobold.

The letting and drinking of blood aside, the plans Vin-ran-olt-hix and his zapovjedniks made that day would have far reaching consequences, although they would take a number of years to come to fruition and were only partly successful.

The conflict known as the Great War ended.

Aed's brother Eanruig died fighting in Russia two years after the war and Nimue left her boarding school to begin her university education.

Some of Vin-ran-olt-hix's underlings based at the priory crypt continued to hunt for the children of King Searc Mael. Others continued to hunt for those with Faie blood in their veins living out in the world. They concentrated on those estranged from their kin and those far enough away from the protective umbrella of the Faie away teams.

As it was in England, so it was elsewhere. 'Elsewhere' was largely in certain areas, areas where there was the highest concentration of those of the blood. These included the Highlands and Islands of Scotland, the northern tip of Ireland, two American states, one area in Greenland, another in Canada and the last above the artic circle in Russia.

A year after Ri-Beag Eanruig's death, Aed's remaining brother Torean was killed. He had survived no less than four assassination attempts in France during the war but a landslide claimed his life as he was leading a war patrol against a group of Kobold reported to be sniffing around Ben Hope up in Sutherland in Scotland.

Investigations by Faie and local police failed to find an underlying cause of the landslide although the Faie investigators had an accurate suspicion.

Raibert's friend Aed became the heir to the throne of the Faie.

By now his sisters had left Scotland, Bana-phrionnsa Elsbeth to her bridegroom and subsequent wedding in Murmansk, Russia, and Bana-phrionnsa Moireach to Canada.

Vin-ran-olt-hix returned to the abbey crypt to get a report as to why Bin-hix had not managed to complete the first part of his mission, the deaths of the children of Searc Mael, and to congratulate him on the success of the other part.

Bin-hix was understandably nervous as he waited for his superior. The last time he had been here, terrible things had happened.

He did his best to make Vin-ran-olt-hix happy, providing fresh food, served in a crystal decanter and comfortable quarters.

"How was Dablingneachd?" he asked, pouring the blood into an exquisite etched glass goblet. The blood was warm.

"Cold," answered Vin-ran-olt-hix, accepting the glass. "It always is. I think every one of us should spend some years living in an Ice Age. It might give us some perspective into how comfortable we are where we are and to make sure we are never sent there again. Would you like to visit?"

"Not especially."

"The only thing stopping you being sent on a little holiday to Dablingneachd is your success with the second part of your mission."

Bin-hix understood.

"We're finding it harder and harder to find them," he told Vin-ran-olt-hix. "Either they're getting better at hiding or they are going further afield. The war didn't help either. Many who were hiding took the opportunity to relocate without being noticed."

"I suspect the latter, which is why I'm sending you …"

Bin-hix caught his breath as his brain rattled through the names of the other worlds Vin-ran-olt-hix might send him to. Please not the World of the Air, nor the World of the Water … I don't want to live in a bubble on a world so alien I can't live a life in it. Goddess Cailleach! Please not the World of the Supercontinent either! Please! I don't want the World of the Dinosaurs but that might not be so bad; at least it is warm but the World of the Ice? Please. No! Can I stay here? I will do better, I promise.

"The only thing that keeps you here in the World of Man," continued Vin-ran-olt-hix, "is the fact that I believe there is still much you can do here."

Bin-hix began to relax, not a lot, just a little bit.

"I want you to move to London and run your kill teams from there. I have a feeling you will be very successful at this, especially with the threat of a relocation hanging over your head."

Bin-hix relaxed some more. He could do that. He liked London with its dark and dirty streets and overcrowded tenements.

What the two didn't know was that Ard Righ Searc Mael was setting up hunting parties of his own, teams dedicated to finding and neutralising the groups of Bin-hix. They would later become known as the away teams.

CHAPTER 10

HIDING HAROLD

*"The speedy gleams the darkness swallow'd,
Loud, deep, and lang, the thunder bellow'd:"*

FULHAM - LONDON - ENGLAND

It was 1940. The blitz was at its height. The German Luftwaffe was trying to bomb the cities into submission.

Harold was terrified. He and his mother had until recently been living in the leafy outer suburbs of Banstead Village some thirteen miles south of Central London, and before that they had lived in a house near Dibden Village which was bounded by the New Forest in the west and Southampton Water in the east. He had been nervous about the noisy, bustling city from the first and that was before the bombs had started.

Also, he had never heard of people evacuating *into* London. It was always the other way round, and mother had actually said they would be safer here!

They now lived in a terraced house half way along a cobbled street off Fulham Palace Road. It was quite a nice house, but Harold didn't think of it as a real home. Home was the detached country house of his youth … but that wasn't there any more.

Harold didn't think he would ever forget that night, not for as long as he lived.

CLOSE TO DIBDEN VILLAGE - ENGLAND

It was the middle of the night and he was alone in a large, dark, over furnished room. He wasn't afraid of the dark or of being alone because he was used to it. When the refugees had come, he and his sisters had moved into one side of their parent's bedroom to make room for them. It was the war, his mother had told him, one had to make sacrifices in times such as these.

In Harold's opinion their house wasn't a large one compared to the house belonging to the family of his best friend along the lane. His parent's home consisted of four bedrooms and three public rooms. One bedroom was the master bedroom where his parents slept (with his baby sisters), another bedroom was at the back of the house where his grandfather had made his abode, and then there were the two upstairs rooms, one belonging to him and the other kept free for guests.

There had always been guests, especially before the war. Some he had been introduced to, they had been strange ... people who talked about things he didn't understand.

One night, as he was snuggling down to sleep, his sisters were downstairs in the middle of their milky suppers, he heard a crash followed by a shout, his father yelling at his mother to go and get him, that he would look after the babies, running footsteps pounding towards the bedroom door.

His mother rushed in. He could hear grandfather's voice bellowing that they should get out through the dining room.

He heard screaming from upstairs and through the door saw grandfather, with a shotgun in one hand and a sword in the other climbing up the stairs faster than he had ever thought grandfather could move, never mind negotiate steps with his hands full.

"Hurry!" his mother pleaded, one fearful eye on the door as she pulled back the bedcovers.

Harold scrambled out of bed and started to look for his slippers.

"No time," said his mother, gathering him up in her arms. He could hear the fear in her voice.

As they left the bedroom Harold caught the faint whiff of smoke where it shouldn't be, and heard the quiet crackling of fire seeking food. He would forever connect fire with death.

Harold's mother ran with him through the dining room and to the wall with the oak panelling. There she put him down as she fumbled with the opening mechanism to the escape tunnel.

There were screams coming from upstairs.

His mother's desperate trembling fingers couldn't work the catch.

Frantic, she pulled him towards a tiny little closet in the corner. Yanking open the door, she shoved him inside, telling him to get right to the back. "Hide right there until I come back," she ordered.

The closet door slammed shut and Harold was in the tiny confined space. It had an earth floor so it was damp. Once upon a time it might have been a larder but now it was merely a tiny, disused space, a tiny, disused, terrifying space.

He was afraid. He was so afraid he thought he might vomit.

He could hear shouts and screaming. Smoke began seeping under the door. Quickly, he pulled some old rags over to plug the gap and as he did, he heard the sounds of something being dragged along the floor.

He heard shouting, rasping voices, and more screaming, then all of a sudden, the screams stopped and were replaced by a high pitched whimpering.

Harold shivered. There was something terrible about the whimpering as if the person knew the end was close. He crawled along the floor to the back wall where the old shelves were where his mother stored old jars and bottles. Trying not to make a sound, he squeezed his body under the bottom shelf.

The dining room went silent and after what seemed like an eternity he decided he couldn't, he just couldn't, stay under the shelf for any longer. He crawled out and made for the closet door. He risked a peek though a tiny space where the old hinge had rubbed away at the wood.

There was a chair in the middle of the room and on that chair his grandfather was sitting. Harold could see streaks of blood running down his face. He watched with bated breath as some black clad people entered the room and recognised a sword blade as it reflected against the ceiling light. He heard a sickening sound like the sound the village's butcher's assistant made as he hacked at mutton bones.

The black clad people left and there was more silence, an empty silence that seemed to last for a lifetime, until … until … he heard a woman sobbing. Mindful of what his mother had told him and shivering with the aftershock of watching his grandfather die, Harold stayed right where he was.

There was a click and the closet door opened and one of the three-time visitors was there, telling him that he was safe and that he was to come out.

Harold crawled towards him and the kern picked him up in his arms, hiding him from the horrors that were the bodies of his grandfather, father and sisters. The whiff of burning wood and charred meat was in his nostrils.

He woke in a strange bed, in a strange room, in a strange house, to the sound of his mother's voice talking to his rescuer.

"The muffle will dissipate soon," the kern was telling her.

"The bodies?" Her voice sounded emotionless, dead.

"Gone to peace," he answered with the traditional response.

"How did they find us?"

"Aislinn, we don't know as yet but I promise you we will try to find out. Perhaps the evacuee family said something in the village and a Kobold spy picked up on it. We might never know. What's important is that we decide what you and young Vero are going to do next."

"I know exactly what to do. We are going to leave this world of Faie with its Kobold and swords and evil goddesses, leave them behind for good. We're going to become human. I am human. Vero is only half Faie. I have family. I will find them. We will become so human the Kobold will never think we are anything else."

"You will be cutting him off from his blood and his heritage."

"Better that than dead."

There was silence for a moment and then a sigh.

"Very well. I will help you," said Raibert. "But I do not like it."

BANSTEAD VILLAGE - ENGLAND

Their time in Banstead Village was brief. Harold's mother, now ostensibly a war widow with a young son, took a short lease on a small semi-detached house. Harold was told to forget that his name had been Vero. He was happy about this, traumatised by the killings, he wanted to forget everything. It had taken him a while to get accustomed to his new name but he found he could get used to a lot of new things if he was determined enough. He went to the local school with all the other little boys and girls (he had been too young to attend school back in Dibden) and said nothing about what had happened.

He might not have said anything to anybody, but he couldn't forget. He had nightmares about his grandfather dying, waking most nights and sobbing his heart out.

One day he came home from school to the news that they were moving again. His mother had been looking worried the last few days, checking the neighbourhood for strangers and forever twitching at the net curtains as if she felt someone was watching them.

It was time to move on.

FULHAM - LONDON - ENGLAND

They moved to a terraced house half way along a cobbled street off Fulham Palace Road … but all was not well.

Not only were there bombs dropping almost every night … there were rumours of blood sucking monsters roaming the streets.

Harold and his mother spent long cold nights in the Anderson shelter at the bottom of the garden. The shelter was a wooden construction, dug into the earth with a corrugated iron cover with a wooden door. Inside there were two long benches at either side and in between there was a table with an oil lamp. At the end there were two small bunks, one for Harold and the other for the little girl next door. It smelt of damp and wet soil.

He hated the sound of the anti-aircraft guns. The noise was deafening and Harold sometimes thought they were the noises made by the dreaded incendiaries hitting the ground and buildings.

School was cancelled, much to Harold's delight and his mother told him they would be leaving London in the near future, moving to the Welsh countryside where there was no blitz. Most of his classmates had already been sent to safety and now he was going too.

However, the near future was not tomorrow and as he got ready for bed that night, not into his pyjamas, but into fresh under things with shirt and shorts on top just in case they had to decant to the shelter, (he had a bag packed with emergency clothes and toiletries), he knew the bombers would be back. They were, if nothing else, predictable.

As he put on a clean pair of socks, his mother was busy making a flask of tea and some sandwiches. The biscuit tin, full of her homemade biscuits, flour, spice, dried egg powder, margarine, honey sent from an ex-neighbour in Dibden, (Harold's mother had not been able to cut herself off completely), and some national dried milk borrowed from next door, was already in the shelter, alongside the cushions and blankets.

The sirens went off with a wail much worse than a roomful of hungry, screaming infants. No one who heard it would ever forget the sound and the fear that accompanied it.

"Harold," his mother was shouting. "Put on your shoes and come down. Hurry!"

Harold did what he was told. Although the shelter wouldn't stop them from being killed if there was a direct hit, it would protect them from flying debris and shrapnel.

"They'll be after the Waterworks again," she was saying as she bundled him into his coat and hat. The Metropolitan Water Works on the other side of the River Thames was a favourite target as was the nearby Fulham Palace, home of the Bishop of London. Walkdens Wharf and its factory was also a popular objective.

His mother was ushering him out the back door, when she looked up and without warning dragged him backed inside.

"Mother, let go," he complained, trying to wriggle out of her grip. "You're hurting me."

"This time we're going out the front door," she said, gripping him so tight he thought his bones would break.

She half dragged him to the door, pulled away the curtain that screened any renegade indoor light from the street (and the eagle eyed Air Raid Wardens), and then bent down to look out of the letterbox.

His mother's terror was transferring to Harold.

"Mother!" he screamed at her.

"Shush," she said. "Don't be scared. Now, I need you to do something for me."

"What's that?"

"I need you to keep a firm grip of your bag …"

"I'm already doing that."

"When I open the door I need you to run as fast as you can down the garden path and through the gate at the bottom. Can you do that for me?"

He nodded.

"Where do I go?"

"Hide in Mr Gregor's garden over the street."

Harold nodded again.

"Where will you be?"

Harold was a brave little boy but his voice was trembling. It was dark, the sirens were blaring and he was absolutely positive he could hear the roar of the enemy bombers above ... on an individual basis.

"I'll be right behind you, I've got one little thing to do," she promised. She opened the door and gave him a little push.

He looked back once as he ran into the dark but couldn't see her.

Taking a deep breath, he crossed the road and reached Mr Gregor's gate. He knew where it was. Mother always pointed it out to him as they passed by. Mr Gregor was the only one with a cream painted gate, easy to see in the dark, even on a moonless night such as this. All the others in the street were green.

The gate was open. Harold went into the garden and pressed his body against Mr Gregor's hedge.

His mother appeared about five minutes later.

The sirens had stopped but he could definitely hear the engines above and the rat-tat-tat of the anti-aircraft guns.

The bombs were falling to the east, towards the docks.

Harold felt they were coming straight for him, hearing them in the distance first and getting louder and louder and louder, closer and closer. He kept looking up, trying to catch sight of an enemy plane and then, caught in a searchlight, he did, for a second, then the bomber banked and the searchlights began frantically searching for it again.

He heard a whistling sound; a bomber had released his stick of bombs. Harold's mother covered him with her body in an attempt to protect him but they knew if a bomb hit they would be dead.

Why aren't we in the shelter? Harold thought this but he knew that for Mother not to take him to the shelter in the garden, the situation must be seriously worse than the bombs.

The explosions were like thunder bellowing.

Shrapnel was falling in huge, red-hot shards and hitting the pavement outside the garden. One piece went through the hedge with a sizzle. A bomb hit close by and the air was full of brick dust, smoke and sparkling slivers of wood and cloth.

They remained behind the hedge, through the raid and the all clear. It was only when the noise stopped that his Mother lifted her head and through the hedge to where their house was burning. The fire engines were there and were putting the fire but she knew there wasn't a hope of saving any of their possessions. The roof was gone, the resulting fire no doubt caused by an incendiary.

Harold was sobbing. "I want to go home."

That first day was a long one. Aislinn and Harold spent hours in the nearest civic centre as they waited for the buses to take them out of the city. In vain did Aislinn tell them that they needed to get to the village of Coombe Bissett, she had family there, but was told again and again that was impossible. If she wanted to go there she and her son would have to make their own arrangements, but she was informed there was a train timetable in the corner.

There was a train to Salisbury leaving from Waterloo Station that evening and despite the warnings from the Civil Defence officer in charge, they didn't get on the buses and departed the centre and walked in the direction of Parsons Green tube station.

Meanwhile, Bin-hix and his team of Kobold had been busy.

They had been on the trail of Harold and his mother since the killing spree outside Dibden, having done their sums and worked out that two of the family had escaped.

They had investigated and one of their operatives had overheard a comment between two ex-neighbours in the village, one woman telling the other about sending honey to Harold's mother in Fulham.

A quick break-in later to find the exact address, the woman would forever wonder why the burglars had stolen her address book and nothing else, and Bin-hix, accompanied by two of his team, had been on his way.

Dusk was turning into night as Harold and his mother left the shelter. The tube station was not far but it was easy to get lost in the blackout so the two, their identity cards saying Alison and Harold Wayfleet (Wayfleet being Aislinn's maiden name) were careful not to get lost, keeping careful track of the white stripes painted on the lamp-posts. There were hundreds of blackout related accidents every week, people tripping, falling down steps, or bumping into things. Angela and Harold had practiced blackout walking so they weren't as disorientated as others might have been. Harold *had* wondered why his mother had insisted they go out walking to specific places when it was dark but he was glad of it now. His mother knew exactly where they were going.

Waiting behind a wall, Bin-hix and his two underlings watched as they exited the centre.

Mother and son passed them by as they walked along the glass-scrunchy pavement but they were concentrating so hard on finding their way they didn't notice.

As he watched them pass and identified them, Bin-hix was holding an ARP Warden's helmet in his hand. Inside was a mess of brains and blood, taken from a man they had found lying injured in an alleyway. Every Kobold needed to eat and London during the Blitz was like a huge butchers shop for a blood eater.

Harold and his mother had almost reached the imposing Victorian Parsons Green station when, all of a sudden they felt the rush of the attack.

Aislinn screamed and Harold took one look at the dark figures, struggled out of his mother's arms and ran straight into the arms of ... a woman.

The black figures melted away into the dark.

"It's all right," the woman said in a curiously lilting accent. Harold knew that accent. He knew that voice. He had met the lady before, in the house at Dibden.

"Lady Elsbeth?" he faltered. "You came to see us when I was little and read me a story at bedtime."

Elsbeth smiled. Harold calling himself little! He was only six and not much bigger than little now!

"You're right," she said. "Well remembered. Now let's get you out of here. Raibert! Take three kerns and try to find those Kobold. Daidh! You help Aislinn. We must go before one of those nosey ARP Wardens comes to investigate. Hurry now."

"Where we going?" asked Harold.

"To a safe place," Elsbeth answered.

"Where's that?" he asked, but she would not say.

CASTLE CRAG - LAKE DISTRICT - ENGLAND

The safe place was far from London, back from whence they had come and further. They remained there while they recovered from their London adventures.

There were no bombs at Castle Crag, or as the Faie called it, Caisteal Creig. It was safe from attack from the air, unless you counted the storms that hit the stronghold in winter.

Harold quite enjoyed his time there. He had friends to play with, and a school to attend (the lessons were different so that made class very interesting), and a language to learn (the old tongue), and the food was absolutely delicious, delicious but different.

He liked being back in the world of the Faie. He felt safe again.

Aislinn however, was adamant in her desire to merge herself and her son out in the world of humankind.

"They know you have links in the southern part of England so you should avoid London, but you would be much safer if you did remain with us, please think about it," said Elsbeth using her most persuasive voice.

Raibert agreed.

"My wife Caoimhe would be happy to welcome you to our home," he told Aislinn. "She gets lonely. I am away a lot of the time."

Aislinn declined every offer.

"We are leaving the Faie," she repeated again and again. "You say we will be safe with you. My husband and father-in-law were not safe, nor my two little girls. We are leaving the Faie."

Eventually a consensus was reached. The split it might be possible, but only in an area safer from the Kobold than from whence they had come.

"Very well. We will help you," said Raibert with a sigh. "But I do not like it."

"You said that last time," said Aislinn.

"Where are you thinking? It should be somewhere close to Faie, for protection."

"We're going to Ayrshire," was Aislinn's surprising answer. "To live with my old Nanny. No one tangles with Nanny."

PRIESTLAND - AYRSHIRE - SCOTLAND

Nanny Wayfleet lived in a tiny cottage that had belonged to her elder sister. It wasn't large but large enough to accommodate Aislinn and Harold who shared a bed with his mother in the tiny room in the attic.

There weren't any bombs here and Harold began to relax, especially after his mother had taken him up to Glasgow one day to see a Mr Jonas Blackthorn.

After the visit, it was as if everything frightening that had happened since the day he had watched his grandfather die didn't matter any more. Indeed, it mattered so little that his brain refused to connect to the memories.

Aislinn Wayfleet began working in a shop in the nearby town of Dervel, or as the locals pronounced it, Dairvel. Harold was soon picking up the valley accent.

Raibert and Elsbeth looked in on them from time to time, but Aislinn had nothing to report and gradually, the number of visits petered away, especially after Elsbeth and her Russian husband were killed by a V-2 in London in 1944.

When Raibert visited the cottage at the end of the war in Europe, the two were gone and Nanny Wayfleet refused to say where.

The search to find them proved futile although Raibert looked for them for a number of years, until that is, the death of his beloved wife and his subsequent promotion to Fo Ceannard of the Army of the Faie in Alba (Scotland). As second-in-command of an army responsible for the protection of the landmass and islands known as Britain, he couldn't go off on what was considered by the king as a number of futile searches for a woman and child, no matter how important they were to him.

He did, however, continue to wonder what had happened. He couldn't say why he thought this but there was a niggle at the back of his mind telling him that young Harold would grow up and play a major role in future events.

CHAPTER 11

MOTHER'S CHOICE

"So Maggie runs, the witches follow,
Wi' mony an eldritch skriech and hollo."

KIRKCUDBRIGHTSHIRE - SCOTLAND

No one would ever call Nimue conventional, whether in the Faie community or out in the world.

After boarding school, she had sat a number of university entrance exams and passed them all with flying colours. Choosing to attend Edinburgh she graduated then went to America where she continued her studies. Her love for the poems of Robert Burns and for the sagas of the Viking Age never diminished.

In America, she didn't accomplish her childhood dream of becoming a professor but did author a number of books. Her main occupation was the tutoring students for examinations. She moved around a lot, as most Faie did when living in human society because of the longevity of their lives and the fact they aged much slower.

During this time she came home to Scotland twice, the first, a quick visit, was for Caoimhe's funeral.

The second, later visit, was more protracted. The Priestesses of Flidais invited her to Teampall Gliocas to become, like her mother before her, and her grandmother and her mother's grandmother before that, a priestess, a Banduri of the Goddess.

She remained studying at Finnich Glen for a number of years before returning to America.

She married late, but as she was of the Faie that did not matter. He was a human, a Professor of Classics. A year after their marriage she became pregnant. Her husband, a man in his sixties, was overjoyed at becoming a father and lived to see his daughter's birth. He was killed in a motoring accident a few weeks later.

Nimue was spooked. A month before his death he had told her he thought he was being followed and had felt sufficiently alarmed to report his suspicion to the police. Convinced the agents of Cailleach had killed him and were targeting her and her baby, she decided to return to Scotland immediately and got in touch with Raibert about when and where to expect her.

It was not Raibert who met her and Aoife at the wharf when the liner docked. It was an elderly kern called Gaisgeil-Chi whom Nimue knew of old.

"I'm to escort you to Caisteal Na Sìobhragan," he told her.

Nimue was instantly on the alert.

"Why? Where's Raibert?"

"There's been an incursion of Kobold," he answered. "Finnich Glen is not safe. The Banduri have gone north while defences are put in place."

"I don't want to go to the castle," said Nimue. "Will you escort us home instead?"

Gaisgeil shook his head, mumbling something along the lines of 'orders are orders'.

"There have been witches seen down there."

"Witches? There's no such thing as witches."

"You know the rhyme … *So Maggie runs, the witches follow, Wi' mony an eldritch skriech and hollo'*. That's what the locals are calling them, dark and cloaked, wandering the countryside, following people walking alone in the dark. The humans don't know what they *really* might well be. Anyway, Raibert is sending an investigative team in and says you can't go there, at least not until he separates fact from fiction, and finds out exactly what the humans are seeing. There's reports of them shouting to each other over the fields at night, otherworldly voices the humans say."

Nimue allowed herself to be escorted to the car but she wasn't happy.

"What about my boxes of books and other things?" she asked. "They're coming by sea."

"I'll arrange their transfer to the castle."

"No. Send them home to the manor. That's where I am intending to live in the future or as soon as Raibert gives me the all clear. We'll not be at Caisteal Na Sìobhragan long. Finnich Glen is no place for babies."

Her old friend Raibert wanted them to stay at the castle and the priestesses wanted her to return to Finnich Glen with them but in the end Nimue got her way (Raibert made the comment 'as usual' when he heard) and travelled, with an escort of Gaisgeil and another kern, to the family manor.

There she began to make a happy home and was content … for a while.

The dreams began when Aoife was six months old.

It took Nimue some time to fully understand what Goddess Flidais was trying to tell her but when she did she cried long and bitter tears.

For Flidais was asking much of Nimue.

She would have to make a choice.

She was of the Faie and therefore had a sacred duty to protect the world from the creatures of Cailliach. So after the tears, came acceptance.

For the next few months, she alternated her time between Aoife and the task Flidais had set her until, at last, she realised it was time. For Aoife's safety and future they must separate.

With loving care, she packed Aoife's belongings into a suitcase. Before she closed the lid she placed a small, carved box on top of her favourite teddy bear, hoping Aoife would be able to keep it and what was inside.

Gaisgeil had two passengers when he left the manor that fine spring morning. When he returned that night, he had one and she was distraught to the point of incapacitation.

It took Nimue weeks to recover (partly) from the loss of her daughter. She rarely smiled except when she remembered recent times past. The task became all-important.

It was a task of two parts.

The first part of the task was the messages, hints, for two to understand in the future. In the dream visions Flidais hadn't been clear about who the two were but when the goddess mentioned *two friends that were once three*, this gave her the clue together with a feeling of rightness. Aed and Raibert were the two, now that the last of their childhood quartet, Caoimhe, was no longer with them.

Flidais made it clear they would have to be understood only by Aed and Raibert and that she would arrange for their transfer when the time was right. Nimue wasn't too happy about this, she liked things with a timetable but was aware that Flidais knew many things she did not.

She set about it.

First … a message so they would know it was she.

Second … another message. As she composed it she was thinking, I hope Caoimhe remembered to tell him before she died. I'm sure she did. She knew how important it was.

Third … the nine magical passwords.

Fourth … the word to activate them. The magical nine would be useless without the activation trigger.

Once these four items were in place, the first part of her task was complete and it was time for the second. She went down the stairs into the basement strong room where the family's wealth had been stored in olden days.

Kneeling over the old kist, she pulled out a green velvet bag and tipped the contents out in her lap.

The first item she picked out was a golden King Robert the Third coin, a 'Lion', known in England as a Crown. She remembered her father showing it to her when she was tiny and had always loved the picture of Saint Andrew on the reverse.

The next items were, in number, nine. They were silver and had all been minted during the reign of King James the Sixth in 1602. They were all 'Thistle Merks' and were as pristine as they day they were hammered, unlike the 'Lion', which had a tiny little notch above the saint's head.

She sat staring at them for a while, before deciding that they were right for the task ahead.

She put the other coins back into the velvet bag and returned it to the chest.

She put the coins in her trouser pocket and turned to look at the wall on which weapons from various times in history and fashion were hanging.

Deciding on one, a large broadsword that according to family tradition the great Prince Artur had carried into battle, she took it down.

It felt right and she felt a tingle through her hand as she held it aloft as if the great warrior himself was giving her his blessing.

She called on Goddess Flidais and informed her she was ready.

Gaisgeil was present when she left the manor house for the last time.

She bade him farewell and blessed him in the old way, as a Banduri of the Teampall Gliocas, with her own blood.

Gaisgeil watched her leave, a cloaked figure walking with steady tread down the drive and through the magical illusion that had hidden the house from prying eyes for centuries.

He knew what he must do.

Nimue had left him with a list of instructions two pages long, that and a parcel.

When he opened the parcel he found it contained a battered, old book. When he tried to read the words inside he found he could not because they were not written in a language he understood.

Written in the flyleaf Nimue had written the words …

> *Gaisgeil my friend,*
> *From Nimue with love,*
> *Keep me safe.*

When Nimue passed through the cobwebby illusion and re-entered the outside world it was as if she had been hit by a blast of sounds. It was rush hour and the roads were busy. Cars and lorries were flashing past her at speeds the previous bearer of the sword would have marvelled at.

The drivers and passengers didn't seem to notice her. She passed through the village of Beeswing and no one spared her a glance.

This was odd. Nimue knew it wasn't every day a woman wearing a long black cloak and carrying a sword passed through.

She assumed Flidais was taking steps to ensure she was not seen, and if she *was*, the watcher instantly forgot.

She passed the old church, crossed the road and struck off across the fields towards the loch.

On the north bank of the loch was the site of a crannag, although most passers-by might be forgiven for thinking it was merely a bumpy hillock in the loch. It was an old site, once used by the Draoidh and their adherents, members of the old religion, a religion that had venerated Flidais.

It was on the crannag that Nimue would start the ritual.

As she clambered over to it, she could feel the muffle forming around her. Neither man nor woman nor child would be able to see through it, an illusion of 'no one here' and forgetfulness.

Muffles were the gift of the High God Jah, to his six children, gifted when their worlds were created.

Some might call them magical, others might call them miracles, but in fact they were the High God's way of ensuring that the creatures under the care and protection of his children were not hurt.

For the Children of Jah who had the duty of protection, the God Ra, the God Lir, the Goddess Nantosuelta, the God Herne, the God Aja, and the Goddess Flidais were not permitted to interfere directly unless they had their Father's permission and their Mother's compliance.

As Nimue came to a halt, the form of Goddess Flidais manifested before her. Absently, Nimue recognised the fact that she wasn't solid, more like half there and half not.

"Will you keep an eye on Aoife?" she asked.

"Two if I can spare them."

"Can you get a message to her? I mean, not now, but when she's old enough to understand?"

"That I can do also."

"Tell her that I love her very much. I didn't want to give her up but I was asked and I did because I love her and want her to *have* a future. If the only way to stop Cailleach is this then I give myself willingly to this task although it frightens me so much I wish I could run away and not look back."

Flidais smiled in a gentle manner.

"You must not be frightened. The kelpies will care for you for as long as you are with them."

"Are you sure?"

"I have asked the favour on your behalf and they have agreed."

Nimue took a deep breath.

She knelt and took the ten coins out of the inner pocket of her cloak.

Her hands trembled as she placed the nine merks on the ground while she retained the gold coin in her hand.

She closed her eyes and prayed to the High God.

"I see my Father, and,
"I see my Mother, and,
"I see my Brothers and my Sisters and,
"I see my people back to the beginning, and,
"They call out to me, and bid me take my place among them in the halls
of Valhalla,
"Where the brave will live forever."

As she finished she held out the coin that was in her hand and bowed her head.

Goddess Flidais floated forward until she was standing over Nimue, arms outstretched, a pillar of protection.

"May Odin give you knowledge on your path,
"May Thor grant you strength and courage on your way,
"And may Loki give you laughter as you go.
"Father! It is time!"

Nimue took a deep breath as she felt the ground shake.

Her hand, the one holding the coin, began to burn as the metal became white-hot.

She screamed in agony but she did not faint. It was as if she was being forced to stay awake, to endure the pain. The waters of the loch began to boil and out of the steam came ghostly shapes of horses with red eyes and flaming tails.

One by one they came over and picked up one of the merks with their teeth; blew on Nimue's hand and the pain disappeared for a moment or two before it returned.

When there were no more merks lying on the ground, Goddess Flidais levitated to float above the crannag.

Nimue heard a crackling sound then she and everything around her burst into flame.

The pain was more agonising than agony.

Out of the water a huge, white kelpie appeared, bringing the loch water with it. He leapt on to the crannag. In an instant the flames were doused and the pain ceased.

"You have passed the test," Flidais announced from her vantage point. "Hurry along now. You know what to do."

Under the watchful eyes of Goddess Flidais and the Kelpie King, Nimue pressed the gold disc that had been the coin into the pommel of the sword and watched the metal melt and form one word ... a name ... 'Aoife'.

"Hurry along," said Flidais. "And we thank you for your sacrifice."

Nimue stood up and walked over to where the Kelpie King was waiting. He bowed his head and in her mind she could hear him telling her to get on his back. Overwhelmed about everything that she had experienced, the normally questioning Nimue meekly did as she was told.

The last she saw of the world as the Kelpie King turned on his back hooves and jumped back into the lake was the face of Goddess Flidais, crying and smiling.

"Until we meet again," Flidais murmured as Nimue disappeared, the waters calmed and the muffle dissipated.

CANDY RAE

CHAPTER 12

CHEST OF SECRETS

"That night, a child might understand,
The Deil had business on his hand."

MILTON KEYNES - ENGLAND

"This is more like it," declared Angela Gillycuddy with a smile. "The flat is so small now that John's walking, and the garden here is lovely."

Alexander Gillycuddy shrugged. "Business is good and it was about time we moved. And I have to say that there's plenty of work for me round here. Everyone's wanting extensions and work done. Where's Susan?"

"She couldn't wait to explore the garden. Was heading straight for the tree at the bottom making murmurs about a swing."

"Isn't seven a bit old to want a swing?"

"Alex! You're *never* too old to want to swing on a swing!"

Alexander Gillycuddy was the owner of a successful building business and Angela had married him last month. She was a widow with two small children, Susan and John. He didn't know much about Angela's life before they had met not long after John was born and had assumed her husband's death was too distressing for her to talk about.

Susan had volunteered the occasional snippet of information about family life when her father had been alive but most of them had sounded too fantastic to believe.

Alexander Gillycuddy's answer had been to ban fairy tales in the house, especially those about evil warlocks, werewolves and vampires. This hadn't bothered Susan. She didn't like to read those kinds of books anyway.

"I'm glad to be out of Birmingham and its dirt and too many people and it's only an hour's train ride away," added Angela. "And before you ask, no, I won't miss my friends. I didn't have a lot of time to make many; we were there so short a time. What's that?"

"The removal van. Better get the kids out of the way. Remember? The park. You were going to take them there. I'll meet you in the café after they've gone."

"Where do you want us to put this old chest?' asked the removal man. "Doesn't say what room."

Alexander turned to look. They were getting to the end of the unloading and he was beginning to wonder where Angela and the children were. He recognised it at once, a battered old tea chest that had belonged to Angela's grandmother.

They had discussed getting it renovated it but the time had never seemed to be right. Perhaps there would be the opportunity here. He must remember to ask the neighbours (when he met them), if there were any traditional cabinet makers in the area.

"In the garage," he answered the gaffer.

"Righty-o! Ray! Jim! Get a move along. This chest is to go into the garage."

"Better get the wheels," said one of the two, Alexander wasn't sure which. "I remember trying to lift it!"

As they got the chest on to the largest sack truck, Alexander, not for the first time, wondered what was inside. He knew it was heavy, the removal men had asked if it could be emptied when they were loading the furniture lorry to come hear but Angela had said no, the key was lost and she didn't want the chest damaged.

Alexander knew his wife had told a porky pie lie. He had seen the key, a small, intricately carved brass one, in her handbag, that very day.

Perhaps it contains some of those memories she doesn't want to think or talk about, he was thinking. One day she'll tell me.

The Gillycuddy family soon settled in. Gran and Grandpa Gillycuddy came to visit and declared that 'the house was lovely' (Gran's words).

Susan went to school and made friends. Her stepfather's business blossomed. Her mother, with some inadvertent help from the toddling John, got the house just right. She was a bookkeeper and did most of her work from home in the garage Alexander made into an office. The car made do with a carport. It didn't seem to mind.

When Alexander made enquiries about renovating the chest, Angela fobbed him off … again. It was the last time he asked.

Eight years passed. The children grew up.

Susan's fourteenth birthday came and went as did John's ninth a few months later. The latter had a party to which no less than thirteen little fiends, at least that was what Susan called them, arrived to 'rearrange' the house and garden.

Susan went to a friend's house for the night after carefully locking her bedroom door. As it was the summer and very hot, she did leave the bedroom window open.

It was when she returned the next morning that she noticed something amiss.

There had been someone in her room.

At first she thought it had been one of John's little friends. Perhaps he had found the spare key her mum had insisted she put in the scrimmage drawer in the kitchen but when she looked the key was there, right at the back under the napkins exactly where she had placed it.

Going back to her room, she checked the window and saw a faint scuffmark on the sill. There had definitely been someone in her room but nothing was missing. What thief would go to all the trouble of entering and not take anything?

"Perhaps he got spooked," suggested Alexander Gillycuddy.

"I was up being sick in the middle of the night," was John's helpful comment. "Perhaps they heard me?"

"We should call the police," said Alexander.

"Has anything been moved?" asked Angela of her daughter. "Susan. Take a good look. This is important."

As Susan scanned the room she got the feeling that there was something more behind her mother's words than she was saying.

When she got to the bookcase she saw it.

"Last year's diary is missing," she said, starting to cry. Last year had been the first that she had kept a diary, a proper diary, like Gran did. She had intended to keep all her diaries and read them to her own grandchildren. In fact, Gran Gillycuddy had started a bit of a craze for keeping paper journals and diaries amongst Susan's peer group, much to the gratification of their English teacher who believed it had been she who had motivated them.

"You sure about that?" asked Angela. Her face was white.

"Absolutely. I'm not going to lose anything as important as that. And it was there yesterday. I know because I put a bookmark inside it, you know, that pretty one we got in the charity shop."

Angela abruptly left the room. Alexander followed, leaving two very confused siblings behind.

"Where they going?" asked John. "Did you see how Mum looked?"

"She was as white as, as a …"

"Ghost," said John. "Susan … I'm frightened."

"There's nothing to be frightened about," she said hugging him.

"What about people climbing in our windows?"

"It was probably just a prank," she answered. "Tell you what … let's go in to your room, make sure the latch is secure and set up some window defences. Then you can come and help me with mine."

John was instantly diverted.

Conversation round the tea table that evening was strained. No one mentioned the police but Alexander told Susan and John that he was going to fit new upstairs windows, a security alarm and an outdoor lighting system. Angela added the fact that a man would also be coming round to assess the viability of fitting security cameras.

They went to bed but Susan, whose bedroom was at the back of the house, was thirsty and couldn't sleep. She got up to get a drink of water and as she passed the landing window, she saw a light in the garage.

At first she thought it was the intruder returning then identified the shadows cast against the open doors as that of her mother and stepfather.

What were they doing?

She never did find out although she looked inside the garage in the morning. Some of the things at the far end, where the chest was, had been moved around but that was all.

The only other thing Susan noticed was that her stepfather was looking rather shell-shocked, and as if he had received information his brain didn't know how to process.

At the end of that week Susan and John learned the house was going on the market.

"Are we going far away?' asked Susan.

"Will I have to change schools?" asked John.

"I don't know the answer to that just now," Alexander Gillycuddy answered. "It depends on how much we can get for this one and what's available."

"John! Eat your greens," ordered his mother. That tone of voice meant the conversation was to cease.

Susan and John discussed the situation over the next few weeks. Their mother and father were jumping at shadows although they were trying to act normally.

"Mum spilt her tea all over the work surface when the postman knocked," said Susan to John.

"And Dad went round the house checking the windows and door three times last night," said John to Susan. "He thought I was asleep but I wasn't. He came right into my room."

"That's not normal," Susan observed. "We're not babies any more. They're treating us like, not children, but toddlers!"

"It's something to do with that night," said John.

"They're trying to hide something scary, like …"

"I heard Dad say it was a devil of a business."

"That night it certainly felt like the devil had a hand in it all," laughed Susan.

"Don't say that word," said John.

"What word? Devil? John, you know there is no such thing."

"And all those locks and chains and the security cameras," continued John. "Susan, do you think they are criminals of some kind and people are after them … or SPIES?"

"I think that is rather far fetched," smiled Susan. "But they're frightened."

"Do you think it's something to do with that old chest in the garage?"

"Why do you think that?"

"I saw Mum in there the other day and when I went in the chest was open and she told me to vamoose."

"Perhaps we should go and look," said Susan.

They waited until their parents had popped out for an hour to a friend's house across the road then giggling slightly (the idea of their parents being spies was too hilarious for words) they slid the bolts of the back door and crept out into the garden, only to be brought up short by what they thought was a figure emerging from behind the chestnut tree.

"Burglar," cried John and scuttled back inside, closely followed by Susan.

They slammed the door and hit the bolts.

"We'd better not tell Mum and Dad we were out," said John. "We'd promised …"

Susan agreed.

On the other side of the back garden wall, the Kobold ground his teeth with frustration. He still hadn't got any proof the two were what he thought they were.

Susan's nightmares began that night.

In her dream, it was as if she was being pulled to the left and then to the right, and by two women!

It was hurting too. Both had a hold of one of Susan's hands and their grip was glutinously sticky.

One of the women had a stern visage and was dressed in blue and the other was quite simply, the most beautiful creature Susan could have ever imagined. Their voices were different, one was strident and one was soft but neither was unpleasant to listen to. Mrs 'Strident' was asking a question over and over again while Mrs 'Soft' was telling her to ignore it.

At the same time as they were talking to her they were arguing with each other.

It was all very complicated.

One of the women gave her arm a sharp tug and Susan woke up screaming. Her mother was with her in an instant, taking her in her arms and rocking her like when she was little.

"It's all right darling. It's all right."

"Did something frighten you?" asked Alexander Gillycuddy who had followed Angela into the room. He had a poker in his hand.

"They're coming to kill us!" cried Susan.

"Who are?" demanded her stepfather, looking serious.

"The nasty people who killed Daddy," she sobbed.

It took a while to get Susan calmed down and begin to doze off but at last an exhausted Angela returned to her own bed.

Alexander was sitting reading. He looked up.

"So, are we leaving Milton Keynes for safer climes?"

"I don't know. I've got an appointment to speak to Mr Anderson on Tuesday morning. He'll know what to do for the best but I have to say that I don't think we'll have to. I'm becoming convinced we're just being paranoid. This all started because of an aborted break-in. Remember, Susan's door was locked and there's not much to steal in a teenager's bedroom. I think they came in, couldn't get out of her room and just took the diary because they felt they had to take something."

"Quite possibly," conceded her husband. "Tell me again what it was like fighting the monsters."

"Alexander! Really! You're worse than a child wanting to hear a bedtime story!"

"And why not may I ask? It's not every husband who learns that his wife is an elven warrior …"

"I'm as human as you are."

"… an elven warrior with a stash of weapons and armour hidden away in an old wooden chest."

"Very well," said Angela, plumping up her pillows and drawing the duvet up to her chin. "A short one though. I'm as tired as a, as a …"

"Kern?"

Meanwhile, Susan was in the land of nod, listening to a soft voice singing …

"On old long syne.
"On old long syne, my jo, On old long syne:
"That thou canst never once reflect, On old long syne."

CANDY RAE

CHAPTER 13

BACK TO THE PRESENT

GODS OF WORLDS

"Should auld acquaintance be forgot and never thought upon,
The flames of love extinguished and freely past and gone?
Is thy kind heart now grown so cold in that loving breast of thine,
That thou canst never once reflect on old-long-syne?"

THE 'PROTEROZOIC'

The World of the God Ra - The First World - The Time of the Air

The God Ra surveyed his world. He was pleased with what he could see.

Time moved slowly here. It was over five hundred million years since 'his' world and what was now known as Earth had become two, but evolution was slow.

It took a lot of energy to 'hold back time'.

The world was now in the middle of what Sixth World geologists had named the Cambrian Era. Early forms of life were swimming in the huge ocean, tribilites, worms, antropods and halluciegenia. Some had ventured on to land, on to the huge continents known as Godwana and Laurentia but the majority of life was in the seas. Ra liked it that way. He loved the plant life and would spend days walking over the land and caring for it.

He knew much about what was happening elsewhere in the Multiverse but as far as he was concerned, there was no need to get involved. To do so might disrupt the delicate balance of permanence he was striving towards.

He instructed his Cuetiachtli, the Druas, not to get involved.

He had decided to continue to exist in isolation.

Old acquaintances, siblings, they were not as important as his world.

THE 'SILURIAN'

The World of the God Lir - The Second World - The Time of the Water

The God Lir surveyed his world. He was pleased with what he could see.

Time moved slowly here. It was over four hundred million years since 'his' world and what was now known as Earth had become two, but he, like Ra, had kept evolutionally development to a snail's pace.

It took a lot of energy to 'hold back time'.

The world was now experiencing what Sixth World geologists had named the Devonian Era. The continents of Godwana and Laurentia were still here but due to continental drift they were moving together and into warmer climes.

There was life in the oceans, in the rivers and on land but it was the oceans and the life within them that were precious to Lir.

Ray finned fish were Lir's favourite animal. They were diversifying and some were becoming quite colourful and beautiful. Lir spent day upon day swimming in the sea with his fish.

Lir knew much about what was happening elsewhere in the Multiverse but like his elder brother, he believed there was no need to get involved. Getting involved would be sure to disrupt the delicate balance of nature on the world he was nurturing.

He instructed his Cuetiachtli, the Sidhe, not to get involved.

He had no need for the company of others. He decided to continue to exist in isolation and not to make contact with his brothers and sisters.

Old acquaintances, siblings, they were not as important as his world.

THE 'PERMIAN'

The World of the Goddess Nantosuelta - The Third World - The Time of the Supercontinent

The Goddess Nantosuelta surveyed her world. She was pleased with what she could see.

Time moved slowly here. It was over two hundred and fifty hundred million years since 'her' world and what was now known as Earth had become two, but evolution was very slow.

The Goddess Nantosuelta had the gift of foresight and she had foreseen what the Sixth World geologists had named the 'Great Dying', the Permian extinction. It had not happened to Nantosuelta's world … yet.

It took a lot of energy to 'hold back time' but she had not been able to slow it down enough to stop the volcanoes.

The continents of Godwana and Laurentia had fused together with other landmasses to form a huge continent the Sixth World geologists had named Pangea.

There were a lot of different types of life, on land, in the oceans and rivers and in the sky, in the shape of insects. Nantosuelta loved them all and fought mightily to ensure their survival.

It took a lot of Nantosuelta's god-energy to keep the volcanoes at manageable levels so that the mass extinction did not happen. She had no time to get involved in what she called the bickering between her younger siblings.

Nantosuelta knew much about what was happening elsewhere in the Multiverse. As with her elder brothers, She did not want to get mixed up in what was happening on the other worlds and because she did not want to, it was not happening. She was in denial but not so much in denial as to forget to instruct her Cuetiachtli, the Siofra, not to get involved.

She decided she needed to devote all her energies to her world so would have to exist in isolation.

Old acquaintances, siblings, they were not as important as her world.

THE 'CRETACEOUS'

The World of the God Herne - The Fourth World - The Time of the Dinosaurs

The God Herne surveyed his world. For the most part, he was pleased with what he could see.

It was over sixty-five million years since 'his' world and what was now known as Earth had become two, and evolution continued at the same pace as the Fifth and Sixth Worlds, with one difference. The extinction events that had occurred in the Fifth World had not happened because Herne had stopped them.

The supercontinent known as Pangea no longer existed. The continents, due to continental drift, were separate and familiar to the geologists and geographers of the Sixth World.

Dinosaurs roamed the continents, descendants of those typified in Sixth World literature, paleontological and geological research, and moving pictures.

It was a beautiful, fertile, dangerous world.

Herne knew much about what was happening elsewhere in the Multiverse and instructed his Cuetiachtli, the Fladhaich, to do everything they could to aid his brothers and sisters in their quest to neutralise his sister Cailleach and his brother Balar.

Old acquaintances and siblings must never be forgotten.

THE 'PLEISTOCENE'

The World of the God Aja - The Fifth World - The Time of the Ice

The God Aja surveyed his world. For the most part, he was pleased with what he could see.

It was over eleven thousand years since 'his' world and what was now known as Earth had become two, and evolution continued at the same pace as the Sixth World, with one difference. There were no Homo Sapiens.

The continents were very like those of the Sixth World although because the sea levels were higher, they looked a lot different.

The world was enduring a series of ice ages. Mammals ruled the land.

Aja knew much about what was happening elsewhere in the Multiverse and instructed his Cuetiachtli, the Ljosalfar, to do everything they could to aid his brothers and sisters in their quest to neutralise Cailleach and Balar, but especially Cailleach.

Old acquaintances and siblings must never be forgotten.

THE 'HOLOCENE'

The World of the Goddess Flidais - The Sixth World - The Time of Man

The Goddess Flidais surveyed her world. She was pleased with what she could see. It was the oldest world, the original and because of this was known as the Anchor of the Multiverse. This was why it was so important and why her sister Cailleach wanted it.

It was also the Time of the Homo Sapien, the Time of Man.

She often felt exasperated with mankind but that was not to say she didn't love them.

She was working with her Cuetiachtli, the Faie, but in an advisory capacity only. She knew, as did her brothers Herne and Aja that any direct intervention by the Gods could mean the destruction of all.

She instructed her Cuetiachtli, the Faie, to do everything they could to aid her brothers and sister in their quest to neutralise Cailleach and Balar.

Old acquaintances and siblings must never be forgotten.

CANDY RAE

CHAPTER 14

PLOTS AND PLANS

"On old long syne.
On old long syne, my jo, On old long syne."

ARDVRECK CASTLE - SUTHERLAND - SCOTLAND

Vin-ran-olt-hix shivered.

It was freezing cold.

Only in Scotland could there be the weather of all four seasons in one day, or in this case, in a single hour.

It had been foggy turning to sunny when he got here and warm for this time of year, then had come the wind, then the rain, and now the snow, that nasty wet snow that soaked through clothes and made your very bones feel damp.

Sometimes Vin-ran-olt-hix wished his Goddess had chosen another world to target. The sub-tropical areas of the Cretaceous for instance would, in his opinion, have been a better choice.

At least his toes wouldn't have been feeling they were about to fall off, quite an achievement for the weather as the Kobold as a race were normally impervious to cold although they did not like it.

He often came to this place. This was where his father had died, and if he was honest with himself, this was the origin of his unswerving loyalty to Cailleach. It had happened a long time ago but the years no longer had much significance to Vin-ran-olt-hix.

His father had fought here, in the area between what were now the ruins of Calda House and Ardvreck Castle. The ruins of the latter rose stark and bleak on the promontory on the east of Loch Assynt. He had always thought the ruins strange, disturbing even, as if the stones were from another age, when witches and warlocks ruled the land. He knew this was pure fantasy but the architecture was odd. What builder in his right mind would place a square tower atop a round one? Still, these walls had lasted for over five hundred years so he must have got something right. Indeed, it might well have been standing today except for what had happened in 1795.

By the end of the eighteenth century, Clan Macleod and Clan Mackenzie had no longer fighting and the Mackenzies had been dispossessed of their estates for their actions during the Jacobite rebellion of 1745.

The castle had been deserted but largely intact and was the location of a Kobold outpost (commanded by Vin-ran-olt-hix's father), until that storm-lashing day when the Faie had arrived.

Vin-ran-olt-hix's father could have run to safety but he had not, lest the location of the nearby and long-time hidden Kobold stronghold was discovered. He and the others with him had fought hard, refusing to give or take quarter, to the death.

The Faie had been victorious.

When Goddess Cailleach had received the news she had been very angry. She directed that anger on the castle, harnessing a bolt of lightning and directing it at it. It had exploded, except for the square tower on top of the round one and some adjacent walls.

The locals believed to this day that a force of nature had accomplished the damage. If they were interested enough to read up on the history they might have found out about a legend that the devil had once lived there. Most people, locals and visitors alike, believed it was just an old ruin, the stones robbed away.

Vin-ran-olt-hix hadn't forgotten. He would never forget. He was constantly plotting on how he could take revenge on the Faie for his father's death, especially revenge on the bloodline of the Faie who had led the enemy, the royal bloodline.

CAISTEAL NA SÌOBHRAGAN - SCOTLAND

Aed Mac Searc Gwrtheyrn Mael, known to his close friends as quite simply, Aed, now Àrd-Righ (High King) of the Faie, took his seat at the top of the table with a sigh. He hated these sessions, preferring to conduct his council meetings in far less formal surroundings than the grand chamber. He also had a gut feeling this one would be protracted. He had been away in Russia during the last month and had only just returned. There was only so much you could manage over the Internet.

It was the room his father had always used for council meetings and every year since his death Aed Mael had been saying he was going to change the location. He never did. There were too many memories.

"We've got a lot to discuss this morning," he began, looking at his notes and smiling at the uniformed lady opposite. "So I suggest we get started. Nansaidh?"

"I have the report from the teams in England," Nansaidh-Chi responded. As Fo Ceannard (Sub Commander) of the Army of the Faie in Alba it was her job to make sure all was well south of the border. "Andaerean-Chi and Ahtna report that their area is quiet, especially after that unpleasantness last year."

"That was *not* your fault," said Raibert, Ceannard of the Army of the Faie in Alba and her superior. "No one knew those Daonna were there and you can't protect those who have distanced themselves so completely from our protection we can't find them."

Nansaidh had to agree but not just Raibert knew she always felt these deaths deeply.

"Everyone else under his team's protection appear to be safe," she continued. "There have been no enemy sightings."

"Which is not the case down in Yorkshire," said Raibert. "I am in receipt of no less than three recent sightings close to a place called Rosedale Abbey. It's located in the North Yorkshire moors."

"With wild and empty areas, even in this modern age," Aed Mael commented. "What do the reports say?"

"Sightings," Raibert replied. "But I got interested so we sent young Orlagh down. She's a recent recruit to our research department."

"We've been introduced. Small with an infectious smile."

"That's Orlagh. She went to the local library and checked out old and new police newspaper reports. There have been a number of missing persons in the area, especially in recent years. When she mapped them out, the centre of these disappearances was Rosedale Abbey."

"Have you sent a team in?" asked Aed Mael.

"Last week."

"Good. As soon as you have more definite information let me know. Next?"

Raibert bit back a smile. Aed Mael had never liked meetings. He remembered him fidgeting in the classroom at Finlarig House when he thought a lesson had gone on long enough.

"We were right about our suspicions regarding young Hamilton Wayman. The DNA results prove it," said Dalach-Chi, the Faie in overall charge of the castle's research facility.

"Should we tell him now?" asked Aed Mael.

"We wait," advised Nansaidh. "We'll need to set up protection for the entire family and we're stretched pretty thin right now."

"He said the other week that his family is coming up for a visit," added Dalach.

"Plan on telling them all together when they arrive," ordered Aed Mael. "Next."

"America," said Raibert. "Information received from Praeceptolem Viho at Lost Eagle Peak." Viho was in command of the Army of the Faie in the Americas. "He believes the vortex there is showing signs of an awakening."

"Any idea about which world it might link to?" asked Aed Mael.

"Not as yet, but if you remember, last time it was the Permian."

Aed Mael's face broke into a smile. "During my grandfather's reign, yes. He used to describe the antics of what came through and the devil of a time they had getting them back. All those little, what do you call them?"

"Elginia," Dalach provided the answer. He had an encyclopaedic memory.

"Right, well, detailed report available? Yes? On my desk please when this meeting is over. I'll phone Kiah this evening. He'll be expecting a call."

Kiah was Aed Mael's son and heir, at present attached to the Army of the Faie in the Americas, in order to gain experience in commanding troops.

"Next."

Raibert caught Nansaidh's eye. She was trying not to smile.

Giol Mac Aboiy Chombaich stood up. He was a member of the Foinaven Mountain and Vortex Guard here in Scotland not far from the castle. The area had, in the past, been described as the 'local route to the sister worlds'.

"The Foinaven vortex is stabilising too," he reported. "Tests on the debris that is blowing through indicate the Pleistocene."

Aed Mael looked towards Zellair-Chi, the Weaponsmaster.

"The team is ready," his voice grated as he rose to his feet. Zellair's voice always grated when he was feeling displeased. "But I still maintain that they are too young."

"We know," said Raibert. "If there was any other way …"

"Oh I know, I know," Zellair responded, waving away the attempt at platitude. "It can't be helped. There aren't enough Daonna. What I don't understand is why our scientists are wasting time testing what comes through the vortexes and not concentrate on finding a way to let pure blood Faie travel through the vortexes. Then we couldn't have to send the younglings through."

"We wish that were the case too," said Raibert. "And they *are* working on it."

"Not hard enough," fumed Zellair plonking his body back into his chair.

"Eh'em," said Aed Mael. "Next."

"The last point is an important one," announced Dalach, standing up to emphasise the importance. "But it is also a worrying one. You will have heard the rumours about the children here at the castle and at Sith Talla?"

There were nods and murmurs from round the table.

"Well, it is not only here. I got one of my assistants, Aven, whom you know is one of the most down to earth people around, to investigate … beyond here and the school. It is *not only* Scottish Faie younglings who are in receipt of these dreams. Scottish Daonna younglings are getting them too ... and as I have recently found out, not just in Scotland … in England … in Ireland … and at Lost Eagle Peak. So, as it appears to be a worldwide phenomena, please may I have some extra staff to help sifting through the reports?"

"Give me a list and I'll sign it off," promised Aed Mael. "Are we finished?"

"Not quite," said Dalach. "I feel we should be asking *everyone* what they think the words inside those dreams *mean*, not just us getting the words and coming to a conclusion. What I'm trying to say is this … someone must have the answer otherwise Goddess Flidais wouldn't be doing this."

"You're sure they are from the Goddess?"

"I am. Some reports say the recipients are hearing her name."

"Agreed," said Aed Mael. "Pursue that line of enquiry."

"I'll add yours and some other names to the list," agreed Dalach.

Raibert caught Nansaidh's eye again and they both laughed out loud. Aed Mael's face was a picture.

ROSEDALE ABBEY - YORKSHIRE - ENGLAND

Bin-hix had survived so far. He admitted to his brother that the reason why had been luck, pure and simple. If he hadn't stumbled across that Daonna family in Birmingham, and the other outside Durham, he was sure he would no longer be alive and kicking.

Their deaths had turned a disastrous few years into years of marginal success.

Unfortunately there had not been a clean sweep of the families but Vin-ran-olt-hix had been so pleased about another 'little matter' that he had accepted Bin-hix's excuse that the teams that had been set up by the late Ard Righ Searc Mael had managed to save three of the children.

In fact, Bin-hix's team had missed the three. Sometimes individual Kobold, especially the inexperienced, got so consumed with the desire for fresh blood thoughts about their primary task went straight out of the window.

The 'little matter' that had so pleased Vin-ran-olt-hix was the information that two very important children had been located, members of a certain bloodline. These children would be a threat to Cailleach's plans if the Faie managed to locate them, threatening enough to give a great deal of aid to the Faie's mission to put an end to Cailleach's plan to defeat her sister and take over the Holocene World.

"When are you planning the trip?" asked Vin-ran-olt-hix, looking past Bin-hix and towards the damp walls of the old crypt. He always tried to avoid eye contact with his underlings.

"Week after next."

"Good. Unfortunately I will not be able to accompany you?"

"That is a shame," Bin-hix lied. "I take it …"

"Our Goddess has summoned me to Dablingneachd," Vin-ran-olt-hix declared with relish and prideful vanity. He loved rubbing noses in the fact that he was Cailleach's most trusted servant. "But that is not to say that I will not know what happens here. Do not fail in this, your most important task yet."

As Vin-ran-olt-hix expected when he dismissed him, Bin-hix departed the little room backwards as a show of respect. He had however, an ulterior motive. It was always prudent not to turn your back on Cailleach's future viceroy.

MILTON KEYNES - ENGLAND

The minivan drew to a halt at the end of the leafy, suburban street.
Bin-hix looked at the street plan.
"It's the third house on the left," he said. "Let's go."

CHAPTER 15

LEGION OF THE FAIE

"Should auld acquaintance be forgot, Tho' they return with scars?
These are the noble hero's lot, Obtain'd in glorious wars:
Welcome, my Varo, to my breast, Thy arms about me twine.
And make me once again as blest, As I was lang syne."

LOST EAGLE PEAK - WYOMING - UNITED STATES OF AMERICA

Fetid and foul was the whistling wind.

Praeceptorem Viho-Chi, Commander of the Legion of the Faie on the North American continent, took a deep breath.

There was no way he could mistake that rancid stench.

They were coming.

"Form battle lines!" he cried. "Ready swords."

They were too close to the unstable entrance to make use of modern weapons. If even one round was fired from a rifle only the Gods knew what would happen.

Possibly the end of everything, thought Viho. The devil within him however wished he and his warriors did not have to rely on cold steel. The hours ahead would be bloody ones and there was something cleaner about a battle using guns and bullets. It was not as personal and up close as a battle with the slice and dice of edged weapons. No matter the weapon however, there was always too much blood.

Spilt battle blood and other spills had a distinct smell, whether Faie or Human, a mix of metal and sweetness together with sweat, faeces, vomit and urine. There was also the taste of fear in the air. Viho knew what fear tasted like, every warrior did.

He pulled down his helmet visor and took a deep breath.

It was time.

He drew his sword.

Immediately to his front the ranks of his warriors tensed as they heard the slither of the blade.

"Shields!" Viho ordered.

The shields thumped down. The noise reverberated through the vortex like a clapper in a cave.

Legionary Accalia-Chi placed her shield into position. To her right Liciana-Chi was mirroring her actions, half a second later as usual, making sure the left edge overlap was wide enough but not so wide that it made them vulnerable. Accalia checked that her shield was overlapping correctly with the tall and rangy Thelonius-Chi to her left.

She had never much liked Legionary Thelonius. He was apt to be supercilious in the company of the female warriors, telling everyone who would listen that they were too small and slight to be of much use against the creatures that might come through from one of the other worlds, but she was glad he was her shield brother *now*. His size and bulk *were* comforting. This was Accalia's first battle and she could do with as much comfort as she could get.

"Draw swords!" ordered Viho.

The stink from the whistling wind was getting worse. Viho felt his throat tighten and fought against the urge to gag.

The enemy was close.

Accalia's insides were a mix of excitement and calm. She felt confident in her abilities as a soldier but didn't know how she would react then it wasn't practice but the real thing.

Tesserarius Mato-Chi, in charge of the left flank centum, Centum X, Accalia's centum, was walking up and down behind the three ranks. His calm voice was telling the warrior-kerns under his command not to panic, and that they must keep in formation no matter what came out of the dark and wind.

"Brace shields," he ordered and again Accalia made sure it was grounded on the floor and in position.

For a fleeting moment Accalia wished she wasn't in the front rank, but that was where Mato had placed her during training. The rank behind was made up of the stabbers and slashers, the warriors who would reach through the front rank with their pikes and their scythe-like long swords.

Accalia had never been much good with a long sword. She was built on a miniature scale and she wasn't tall or long-limbed enough to have reach enough. The front rank swords were stabbing implements, wide and short. The rear rank was made up of the specialists, archers and the like, but they could fight with the wide-bladed front ranks as well as any other kerns.

The kerns were waiting for the command that would tell them battle was imminent.

The stench from the vortex had got so foul that some warriors began to cough.

Accalia took short breaths in a vain attempt to evade the stink. Viho was no longer the only one trying not to be sick.

She had heard the phrase about ground shaking beneath feet and now it actually was.

The dirty air felt oppressive, as if all the nastiest air from the parallel world at the other end of the vortex was trying to force entry into the oxygen rich world protected by the Faie.

"Brace, Brace, Brace!" Mato's voice rang out. Accalia tightened the muscles in her shield arm and took a firmer grip on her sword hilt. "Remember middle rank; get under the shields every chance you get."

Round the corner came the enemy.

In the rear ranks, the archer-kerns fired. Arrows whirred but there were too many of the enemy for them to do more than fell a small percentage.

The creatures of the enemy vanguard charged and quickly reached the shield-wall.

Thelonius grunted. "Spriggan," he hissed between clenched teeth.

Accalia staggered as a heavy body crashed against her shield. Although she had imagined what a Spriggan would be like up close, she hadn't expected it to be *this* big and heavy. The Spriggan's face was coarse and sweaty, and its eyes were glinting with what she imagined was malevolent glee. She leaned forward and thrust her sword out and up as she had been taught during training.

She felt as if she was an actor in a slow motion movie.

The Spriggan's eyes became dull as its body buckled and slid away from her sword.

"Good," yelled Thelonius. "Keep it up girl!"

As more Spriggan reached the wall of shields the line wavered as some warriors were forced to fall back. One and then another buckled under the combined weight of hundreds of enemy who were pressing against them. Accalia was conscious of the second rank pushing at her back in an effort to keep her upright.

A mouth full of blackened teeth appeared over her shield and Accalia looked into what she imagined the gates of hell might look like. The drool from the Spriggan's mouth splattered over her face. It stank.

Her sword arm moved upwards stabbed at its neck. That head disappeared with a howl of pain but other heads kept on coming.

She felt something grasp at her ankle and attempt to pull her forward and out from the shield wall. She kicked and the something disappeared.

She glanced to her right. Liciana wasn't there any more. In her place was another kern who was trying to force his shield into the gap where she had been.

We have to hold. If we don't this part of America will be infested with … these … and whatever else comes out of this maelstrom.

Suddenly, the pressure eased and the Spriggan warriors fell back a couple of metres. She could hear them screaming as they formed back into their ranks and psyched themselves up for another attack.

"Fill the gaps!" yelled Praeceptorem Viho. "Check your shields! They'll be attacking again!"

The second charge was more ferocious than the first.

The battle crazy Spriggan came thundering towards them. Accalia braced. One Spriggan leapt at the left side of Accalia's shield with such force it shattered. She staggered back, as she fell, managing, (she never understood how) to bring her sword down on the beast's shoulders. She felt the scrunch as the blade hit bone. The Spriggan staggered and fell, landing on top of her. The weight knocked her to the ground but somehow she managed, more by luck than design, to keep the fragment that was all that was left of her shield above her body.

"Hold on," yelled Thelonius. He leapt at the Spriggan, forcing it to concentrate on him rather than Accalia. His sword came down. There was a gush of thick blackish blood and the Spriggan was dead.

Accalia could smell the metallic blood. She tried to crawl away but it was impossible to find a route through the legs. The fighting was too close.

"They're faltering! Drive them back!" cried Viho.

Gathering their courage, the Faie battle lines solidified.

"Advance!" yelled Viho. It was the command the Spriggan were not expecting. They faltered some turned their heads, looking to their rear for orders. The orders did not come.

The Spriggan became as silent as a ghost army.

"Advance!" repeated Viho.

"The fight's not in them," observed Thelonius, surveying the scene from the vantage point of his superior height. "They're retreating!"

The roar from the Faie was so loud Accalia felt her ears pop.

"Thank the Gods," said Accalia, managing to raise her upper torso although she couldn't quite manage to stand. Her legs felt like lumps of jelly. In front of her was a body. It was Liciana. Her lifeless eyes were open but they could not see.

The two had been friends since the morning they had arrived at Chaill Iolaire Stùc to start their training four and a half years ago. Accalia burst into heartbroken tears of loss. They had spent evenings talking about the future, of how brave they would be in a fight and how one day they would marry, have children and about how they would smile when their daughters went to Chaill Iolaire Stùc to follow in their mothers' footsteps.

Accalia would have to face future dangers on her own, and war wasn't glorious, not at all, and the heroes? They were the dead.

STRONGHOLD OF GODDESS CAILLEACH

Crash! Crash! Crash! Bumpy-bump!

The vase spun through the air and crashed against the wall.

Because Cailleach was an immortal and was in possession of abilities not constrained by mortal rules, the vase didn't just smash; it shattered into millions of flaming smithereens and actually dented the stone.

The flowers were history.

As each miniscule shard connected with the stone it popped so loud a herd of aurochs three miles away stampeded.

The inhabitants of Dablingneachd covered their ears in a vain attempt to block out the noise. Goddess Cailleach's brother, the God Balar, cringed. Cailleach's temper had always been bad and this setback, as with others before it, had brought out her worst attributes, ambition, temper and vindictiveness. He wondered who she would kill this time.

Thank the High God Jah this time there were prisoners. Last time one of her plans had failed she had taken her temper out on *him*, her brother, *and* murdered over a hundred of his Spriggan, He had lost too many of them already today.

Balar mourned their loss. He had loved them as only a God could but, and it was a big but, he loved his sister more.

He loved her but he feared her. She took the meaning of unpredictable to a new level. He knew that if she had to pick between success and him, she would choose the former. Despite this he couldn't help but follow her, she was his life.

Their failure at Lost Eagle Peak was a setback. The Faie warriors hadn't followed the Spriggan into the vortex as Cailleach had planned.

Instead, they had recognised the retreat for what it was. A trap.

The God Balar wondered what Goddess Cailleach would do now.

Something bad, of that he was sure.

CHAPTER 16

KILL BY FIRE

"Should auld acquaintance be forgot, and auld lang syne?
And surely ye'll be your pint-stoup! And surely I'll be mine!"

MILTON KEYNES - ENGLAND

The street was as quiet as a graveyard in winter as the six figures moved towards the third house on the left.

It was similar to the rest of the houses in the road, built in the early 1970's, with two public rooms and a kitchen on the ground floor and three bedrooms upstairs, although this one had another bedroom built over the garage and a sunroom extension at the back.

The Gillycuddy family would have recognised the house.

Bin-hix had explained the plan to his underlings in detail. They all knew what to do, even the driver of the van, who was Spriggan, not Kobold and thus not the brightest penny in the purse.

"You got the oil?" whispered Bin-hix.

With difficulty, the Kobold lifted a drum from under his cloak so that Bin-Hix could inspect, and so did the other three, also with difficulty.

"I told you four gallons should be enough." Bin-hix's whisper was tight with anger. "That is far more than is required."

The Kobold nodded then shook his head, indicating that he had done exactly as ordered. "Four gallons each," he said. "I've got the receipt to prove it."

"*One* gallon high grade cooking oil each," Bin-hix hissed. "Four gallons *total*."

Bi-hix couldn't understand how Id-hix had managed to botch the calculation but let it lie. There would be time to delve into their stupidity once the deed was done.

One Kobold began to walk casually up and down the road, keeping to the shadows and ready to stop interference while the rest slipped into the garden and hoped the security lights weren't switched on. They weren't. The new owners thought the amount of security was excessive and had disconnected over half of the intruder warning systems.

Bin-hix made a quick prayer to Goddess Cailleach for her kindness in arranging the disappearance of this inconvenience although he knew in his heart of heart she had had nothing to do with it. Still, where Cailleach was concerned, it was better to be safe than sorry.

The five made for the back garden, as silent as the black wraiths of death, which of course, they intended to be.

The rewards for killing this family would be extensive and of bountiful bloodiness.

Bin-hix opened the back door to the house himself. That was the wonderful thing about these old doors, they were a thief's paradise; so easy to open with a certain type of speciality tool. Bin-hix possessed a number of these tools.

They tiptoed round the ground floor and the bottom part of the stairs, spreading the oil around liberally with special attention to any escape routes at the doors and windows.

"Go deal with the outside," Bin-hix ordered Id-hix who nodded and went to pour what remained of his oil (which was a lot) outside the walls. Once the drums were empty Bin-hix ordered the Kobold outside.

"Two minutes," he told them, lighting the fuse and placing it on top of the cooker after switching on the gas hobs.

Bin-hix then departed, closing the door behind him and dropping the match on the top step. He slipped on the oil and cursed. As they all ran down the side of the house and through the front garden, Bin-hix was positive flames were at his heels although the oil hadn't ignited yet.

There was a rush to get through the front gate but at last they were on the pavement and scrambling into the van.

It took off immediately, gears crunching as the Spriggan driver tried to get up to forty miles an hour in five seconds. He didn't manage the forty but was close. The van turned off the road when the house exploded.

During the same night, in two other locations, there were attempts to kill Faie and Daonna by fire.

In the first, in Bedford, the attack was made on the wrong house, one with a bright yellow door, the arsonists not being aware that the target house had recently painted theirs a dull blue, and in the second, also in Bedford, the family had woken up, and seeing strange figures in their back garden, phoned the police.

Bin-hix was pleased with his work and even more pleased when he found out about the other two failures.

On their drive back to Rosedale Abbey, he also managed to work out why Id-hix had brought so much oil. Until recently In-hix had served the goddess in a remote area in the north of Scotland where the locals had clung on to the old ways, weights and measures.

In that hamlet a gallon was a gallon but a gallon, when measured, was equal to over four standard gallons.

There was a ditty Bin-hix knew from his childhood, before metrification. 'Two cups make one pint and eight pints make one gallon.'

In-hix had another ditty. 'Two chopins make one joug and eight jougs make one gallon', adding that he had loved drinking his daily blood ration from a pint-stoup and that he wished other blood distribution places provided their clientele with those nice big beer mugs.

The breakfast news the following morning was full of the story about the 'gas explosion'.

Consensus was that the cause was a gas leak.

In their new home, the Gillycuddy family were shocked when they realised where it had happened.

Susan Gillycuddy was glad the people who had bought the house from her parents the previous year had not been there when the explosion had occurred.

John Gillycuddy wondered if his stepfather might be persuaded to take him to what the reporters were calling the 'disaster site' to have a look.

Alexander was relieved the four of them had not been in the house, and like his stepdaughter happy no one had been hurt. He didn't think he would have forgiven himself if another family had died because he and his had once lived there.

Angela decided to make some contingency plans. She went downstairs into the cellar where the chest had been put when they had moved in.

From its depths she extracted a dagger and a wrist knife.

CANDY RAE

CHAPTER 17

AULD LANG SYNE

"We twa hae run about the braes, and pou'd the gowans fine;
But we've wander'd mony a weary fit, sin' auld lang syne.
We twa hae paidl'd in the burn, frae morning sun till dine;
But seas between us braid hae roar'd sin' auld lang syne."

CAISTEAL NA SÌOBHRAGAN - SCOTLAND

Dalach-Chi was in charge of research and development at the castle. He was a mathematician, a physicist and a geologist, and was the leader of the team who were working out how the vortexes worked and, more importantly, how to predict when the routes to the other worlds in the Multiverse would be open and when they would not.

Other people within the department were in the middle of a conundrum of research of a different variety, most definitely not scientific.

Three of these individuals were Orlagh-Chi, Torian-Chi and Aven. The two Faie had degrees in literature, specifically Scottish Literature. Aven's expertise lay with Mediaeval Scottish History.

Visitors to the castle would make comment about this apparent anomaly. They thought it strange that in the middle of scientific research about how to keep Goddess Cailleach at bay (working out practical ways to do it), that an entire corner of the main lab was filled with musty books of varying ages and indeterminate providence. The large numbers of whiteboards attached to the walls in this area were not filled with scientific formula and mathematical calculations, as was the case on every other board inside the large room, but with words of poetry.

On the boards were written many different versions of Robert Burn's *Auld Lang Syne.*

The trio's investigation had lasted over a month, ever since the full extent and import of the dreams had been realised. It wasn't every day that Goddess Flidais inserted cryptic messages into the minds of over a hundred children and adolescents. The last time had been over five centuries ago. Then it hadn't been the *Auld Lang Syne* by Robert Burns but the *Sweit Rois of Vertew* by William Dunbar. That message warning had been the precursor of dire and soon to come danger, and had led to a time of great peril for the Faie. Everyone was sure another 'now as then' time was approaching.

Orlagh-Chi looked up from her perusal of a dusty tome with a sigh of pure frustration.

"No matter which way I look at it, I can't find a connection."

"Neither can I," admitted Torian-Chi, "and I've been hunting through the earliest editions we've got." He closed the book with consummate care. It was very old and extremely precious.

"What about the Robert Ayton version?" asked Orlagh.

Torian shook his head. "Not a hint and I've analysed his, and all the other extant pieces of the earlier ones. Nothing. Dad. Nada. Zip."

Orlagh looked at the largest whiteboard. She read out the top lines …
" *'On old long syne my Jo, on old long syne, That thou canst never once reflect, on old long syne.'* They're the most frequent words, or a close version of them. I wonder why those words specifically?"

"Every arrangement and every permutation is being heard," warned Torian. Orlagh could get fixated on one area if she thought she was getting somewhere. He knew they were still at the 'keep an open mind' stage of the investigation.

"But that is the phrase that comes up the most often. I'm also wondering if we've got the spelling right too. Some of the kids who've been getting the dreams are very young."

"What's worrying me more that spelling is that although it's *usually* those lines, it's not always," mused Torian. "And why does Robert Ayton's version pop up so often? It's not that different from the others, except the sixteenth century one of course. What's so important about *that* specific one?"

He looked over to the third and oldest member of the team, and raised an eyebrow in enquiry.

For years, Aven had been trying to link Scottish history, tradition and folklore. He had a firm belief that the answers were all there to be collated and interpreted.

"Apart from the connection of Rabbie Burns's *Auld Lang Syne*, not helped by the fact that Burns wrote a number of variants, notably the one in the dreams, but also the traditional version, *Old Long Syne*, to whit, the verse from Robert Ayton or perhaps the words of Francis Sempill, as printed in the 1711 edition by James Watson, the evidence points to no connection with what we're looking for," said Aven, not even looking up from the papers in front of him.

Orlagh blinked as she tried to assimilate the rather confused ramble. "Actually, we're not sure *what* exactly we *are* looking for," she said, half to herself. Every time she asked this question of the other two she was told they would know it when they found it, an explanation that didn't fill her with a whole lot of confidence.

Problem was, Goddess Flidais, if it *was* she who was behind the dreams, had a history of giving her kindred obscure hints and in all likelihood the Auld Lang Syne hint would turn out to be the same, obscure to the point of impossible.

"Burns knew about the earlier versions, there's documentary evidence to prove it," she pointed out.

"He knew," agreed Torian. "Even wrote about it. Claimed two of the stanzas were his own but the rest he had taken from traditional oral and written versions."

"So we've got nothing," sighed Orlagh.

"Not so fast," uttered Aven, sporting a smile. "I might just have something."

Orlagh's voice might have been forgiven for sounding rather dubious. "Another version?" she asked in a snippy voice.

"No, it's from a book first published in England in 1694."

"A London edition of Robert Burns?"

"The title is, and wait for it, Scotch Presbyterian Eloquence Display'd, Or The Folly Of Their Teaching Discover'd From Their Books, Sermons, Prayers: Interspers'd With Some Genuine Adventures, In Love et C. The authors are a Gilbert Crokatt and John Monro, I can't find out much about their lives but there is a distinct possibility these might not be their real names."

"That's some mouthful," Orlagh noted.

"The relevant passage is this," continued Aven. "Did you ever hear tell of a good God and a cappet prophet, Sirs? The good God said, Jonah, now billy Jonah, wilt thou go to Ninevah, for Auld lang syne? It's a salacious work, a book of its time. The words are reported to have come from a sermon."

" 'Cappet' means? Remind me someone," pleaded Orlagh.

"Contentious, petty," Torian answered. "But I don't see …"

"Ninevah," she said then. "Now where have I heard that before? No. I can't remember."

Torian blinked.

"I can. It was an ancient city in what is modern-day Iraq," he said.

"It was, but I believe the minister was quoting from the bible. The quote would have come from a protestant sermon and the minister would have been using, probably, one of two bibles, either the King James or the Geneva," explained Aven.

"Don't keep us in suspense."

"The relevant verse in the King James version here in the library is, Out of that land went forth Asshur, and builded Nineveh, and the city Rehoboth, and Calah. The Geneva 1560 version's equivalent goes like this, Out of that land came Asshur, and builded Niniueh, and the citie Rehoboth, and Calah."

"Niniueh," breathed Torian but Orlagh didn't hear him.

"Which version would the nameless minister have used in the sermon?" she asked.

"He would have known both. The Geneva translation was generally used until the Kirk adopted the King James Bible in 1611. The Scots version came out twenty-two years later but the Geneva Bible would have been in use until the end of the century. Books were expensive in those days."

"Niniueh," repeated Torian. His breath was deepening with excitement.

"Precisely," agreed Aven. "I was wondering … especially with the use of syne …"

"If the dreams about *Auld Lang Syne* are linked to the prophecy. That's a big leap, but ..."

"You got anything better?" asked Aven with a grin.

"What prophecy?" asked Orlagh.

"During the first half of the Fourteenth Century here in Scotland," began Torian. "There were a number of languages being spoken. The word syne is derived from the Anglo Saxon, a language that was spoken in the northern part of the Kingdom of Northumbria. Some linguists think syne derives from the word sith, others seine, syn or sethen, although I discount the last one. During that time, like now, a number of Faie and Daonna were dreaming about a rhyme that included the word 'syne', that's why there might just be something in all this."

"Tell her about the prophecy," ordered Aven.

"I can do better than that," he answered, getting up from his chair and walking towards the door that separated the facility from the library. He returned a few minutes later, carrying a large, dingy book of indeterminate age. This he set down on the table before sitting down himself, at the same time pulling on a pair of white conservation gloves.

"It's been a long time," he told the other two, opening the book and running his hand down the index. "Here it is."

He began to look for a certain page. The pages were so old the vellum was crackling in its fragility.

"Right. An ancestor of mine wrote this book in 1345. In *his* grandfather's time there was an attack by Cailleach and Balar here at the castle, at Sith Talla and at Sabhailte gu caladh reidh."

"All here in the Highlands," noted Orlagh.

He was gazing into space as he spoke, as if he had learned the words by rote, which he had, in his childhood.

"They were beaten off and after the Goddess Flidais had seen the numbers of dead Faie and Daonna on the battlefields she was distraught. She called out for her father, High God Jah and he came.

" 'Father' she cried. 'How can I stop Cailleach and Balar from killing my children? What can I do? Will you please stop it?' "

"And High God Jah said not, that he could not, that it must play out until the end, but he did grant her a boon, a sliver of light at the end of the road she and her children must take …"

"The prophecy," said Orlagh. "I remember reading about it. What does it say?"

"I'll read it out to you," agreed Torian. "The language is Old Faie, how we used to speak … 'agus thig i gu bhith a rèir a 'chòigeamh lagh nan uile gum bi trì de na sìth a 'tighinn beò agus thig sin gui crìch agus bidh seo a 'tachairt aig Sith Niniueh nuair a tha trì agus còig gabh pàirt a bhith nad aonar a dh 'aindeoin dithis'. It translates as … 'And it will come to pass, that according to the Fifth Law of All, that three of the peace will prevail, that an end will come. This will happen at Sith Niniueh, when Three and Five combine to become One to defeat the Two.' That's it."

"So where's this Sith Niniueh?" asked Orlagh.

"No one has been able to find out," Aven shrugged. "Up until today

I've always thought the whole thing a myth."

"It still might be a myth," warned Torian, "but my gut's telling me that it's not and that we should be trying to find it."

FINLARIG HOUSE - PERTHSHIRE - SCOTLAND

In the comfortable drawing room of what Raibert called his 'ancient ancestral pile', five Faie were sitting in front of a roaring fire sipping a fine Glenmorangie.

"A treat for us all," Raibert had said, filling the crystal glasses.

"And I thought you were going to open the Balvenie in honour of my visit," grinned Aed Mael.

"I'm keeping *that* for a *very* special occasion."

"Obviously a visiting king is not special enough," Aed Mael laughed, sipping at the twenty-one year old claret-wood malt. "But this is nice, very nice." He took another sip. "In fact, it is exceedingly good. How many bottles do you have?"

"This is the only one of that vintage," answered Raibert with a sigh of deep regret.

"In that case, I'd better savour it," opined Aed Mael as he settled back into the armchair on his side of the fire.

Marsail, Fionn and Daidh, Raibert's other guests, were also quietly sipping, savouring the whisky's flavour and body.

"Why's it called a claret-wood?" asked Marsail.

"It spent a considerable amount of time in a cask that once held claret wine," answered Raibert. "There are not many of them left."

"Cost you a pretty packet?" queried Daidh with an arch look. The two were old friends.

Raibert could only smile in agreement.

"Do you remember when we were lads?" began Aed Mael, as he often did after a couple of drams here in the home of his childhood.

Marsail, Fionn and Daidh settled down to listen to the stories.

"How could I forget?"

"Do you remember that time when the two of us escaped from Nanny and ran up and down the hills in our underwear? Nanny was incensed, not that we were wearing underwear but that we'd gone without our socks and shoes?"

"I do," answered Raibert, with a wince as he remembered the resulting punishment. Nanny Ceiteig had belonged to the school of 'Gie a bairn his will and whelp his fill, and neither will dae weel'.

"And that time we paddled in the burn, all day. I thought I would be on bread and dripping for a week never mind the two days."

"And Caoimhe sneaked us some bread and jam."

"And was caught."

"Then Nimue told Nanny it was her idea."

Raibert's eyes were suspiciously bright, as they always were when he thought about his beloved wife.

Aed Mael noticed and decided to move the conversation on.

"But enough," he said. "All this *paidlin' in the burn* stuff is taking me back to one of our present problems, Burns and the *Auld Lang Syne* dreams."

"Would you care for another dram?' Raibert asked Daidh.

"You sure?"

"For old friends, nothing is too good," declared Raibert in a dramatic voice.

"Less of the old please," growled Daidh, but his eyes were twinkling.

It was as Raibert was thinking about a suitable reply when the telephone landline rang with the news about the fire in Milton Keynes.

"Yes," the others heard Raibert's end of the conversation.

"Five?"

"Yes. Send the investigative team in."

"Three weeks you say? Well, they might not have known."

"Where?"

"Yes. You've done well. Keep me in the loop. Goodbye."

He put the receiver down, turning to his expectant audience.

"Fun time's over. Three separate attacks on homes being lived in or recently vacated by, Faie and Daonna."

"How many?" asked Aed Mael.

"A family of five quite innocent and unconnected to us, humans, in a house in Bedford. They'd only been living there a week, hadn't finished their unpacking. We didn't know the family that left the house were connected to us until Andaerean-Chi alerted us this morning, never mind the fact Kobold had traced where they were living."

"Why wasn't the house put under observation?"

"It was but Andaerean had tagged the building as a yellow risk, quite rightly, because the family he's protecting had moved out a number of weeks ago. He's understaffed too, especially since Hrolfr-Chi and Kailen-Chi were transferred back here."

"What has he managed to find out?" asked Aed Mael.

"Only that a white van with dark writing painted on the side was seen at the scene and some people in dark clothes were clocked exiting the said van shortly before the fire started. The police are treating it as an arson attack. Andaerean did mention that there have been reports of sightings of a similar van or vans in an area close to Southampton, plus three times in the village of Cropton and in Pickering too, that last is multiple sightings."

"Yorkshire again. That can't be a co-incidence," noted Marsail. "Pickering is close to Rosedale Abbey, where Orlagh mapped out those disappearances."

"Twenty minutes, give or take and Cropton is half that," answered Raibert, checking the map on his mobile before answering. "The Kobold are getting braver, either that and there's more of them. I'm sending a team into the area. We have to find out what's happening and Andaerean needs more help."

"I'll take make contact with Jamie and see if he's heard anything," offered Fionn.

"Yes. Do that."

Late the following evening Raibert received an interesting snippet of information.

Three butchers in Pickering had reported in the local media that sales had been increasing steadily over the last year, especially offal. Armed with that information, the team member had decided to investigate further because she knew Kobold ate a lot of raw meat, the bloodier and more liverish the better.

The butchers had informed her that they delivered to a certain restaurant once or twice a week. She went there and looked at the menu. No offal was on offer.

She had then visited the nearest slaughterhouse and found that their insurance company had insisted they upgrade their security system due to a number of thefts.

When she had asked what had been stolen the man in charge told her that he had been surprised that they hadn't taken the expensive meats but had taken the contents of the vats of blood. The thieves had employed lorries disguised as fuel tankers to extract the liquid.

"It happened during the working day," he had explained. "We all thought they were delivering the fuel for the furnaces which are down that end."

As Fionnuir-Chi had walked away she had been moved to wonder how the Kobold thieves had managed to hold back their urges in the presence of so much killing and blood.

For Raibert, this information was confirmation. The Kobold base in that part of England was at Rosedale Abbey, or close to it.

We'd better get a good nights sleep," said Aed Mael, sipping at the last of his malt. "Raibert! What time's the car ordered for the morning?"

"Jamie will be here at ten," answered Fionn. He had arranged the transport. It was time for the young man to get a glimpse at the world he was about to enter.

"Better make it eight. I need to get back to the castle as soon as possible. Raibert?"

"I'll be staying," said Raibert. "I need to have a conversation with young Hamilton Wayman and get everyone organised. I can do that as well from here."

"Right-o," agreed Aed Mael, placing his glass down on to the table. "I'm for bed."

CAISTEAL NA SÌOBHRAGAN - SCOTLAND

Torian-Chi, Orlagh-Chi and Aven had been busy trawling though the library shelves containing the early records for, and Orlagh had been counting, the eleventh time.

They found any number of interesting facts and fiction but nothing that led them to believe they had found anything of importance relating to the dreams of the woman's voice, singing, *'On old long syne my Jo, on old long syne.'*

Orlagh had come up with the Arthurian legend about the Lady of the Lake. In some versions, the name of the aquatic sorceress was Vivien or Niniane, or Nimue but they could find nary a link between that and the verse.

Torian had come up with some Anglo-Saxon references to syn, sin and sith, meaning afterword or since. He was continuing to pursue the language trail.

Aven was getting somewhere. Although he could find no trace of a link between *'Sith Niniueh'*, and *'On old long syne my Jo, on old long syne'*, he had had some luck tracing place names.

He had begun with the three words, 'syne', 'sith' and 'Niniueh'. As expected, he had no luck with the last, 'syne' wasn't much better, but 'sith' yielded a number of results, too many. They had decided to concentrate their search to the Highlands. The north of Scotland had always been more sparsely populated than the rest of the country; it had been here that Cailleach's previous attacks had been concentrated; and recent intelligence was that her hideout in this world, Daingneachd, was

105

in the area.

The Scottish Gaelic word sìth/sìdh was pronounced shee. Aven had found out that when talking about ancient place names it often meant a 'fairy hill'.

Aven was narrowing down the search parameters.

He read them out to his co-investigators …

"Glenshee … 'glen of the fairy hills'; Sìdh Beg … 'small fairy hill' and Sìdh Mòr … 'big fairy hill'; Schiehallion … 'fairy hill belonging to the Caledonians'; "Ben Tee above Loch Lochy … Beinn an t-Sìth 'the fairy mountain'; Sìthean Mòr … 'big fairy hill'. It's on the Island of Handa; then there's Sìdhean Dubh, which is the 'black fairy tor' on the Isle of Skye; and Sìdhean an Airgid, 'fairy hill of the silver' on the Isle of Lewis; Sìthean a' choin bhain, the 'fairy mountain of the white dog' in Easter Ross. And there's more."

"I think that's enough to be going on with," said a voice. "It'll take us weeks to investigate them all. And there are more pressing matters … in Yorkshire."

It was Aed Mael.

FINLARIG HOUSE - PERTHSHIRE - SCOTLAND

It was the next day and Raibert was getting ready to go and join his away teams when his mobile rang. It was Aed Mael.

"I've just heard from Fionn with some confirmation regarding Yorkshire," the king told Raibert. "Two vans have been sighted heading towards Rosedale Abbey and another departing from it. Nansaidh thinks they've got wind of the fact we're on to them and are gathering in their warriors."

"Have they found anywhere where their base is exactly? It's an old mining area. Old mine workings or shafts?"

"There is any number of old industrial sites. I've had kerns out all day looking, disguised as hill walkers. They say no trace. Raibert, it has to be somewhere inside the village itself. We're beginning to think it's actually the site of the village churchyard. The village church was built on the site of a small Cistercian nunnery, twelfth century we think."

"Did it have a crypt?"

"Nothing in the records."

"But that's not to say it's not there," said Raibert. "My gut is telling me …"

"Mine too."

"Okay. Send the rendezvous details out to everyone."

"Time?"

"Midnight tomorrow."

"Wilco. Over and out."

CHAPTER 18

VAMPYRE CRYPT

*"And there's a hand, my trusty fiere! And gie's a hand o' thine!
And we'll tak' a right gude-willie waught, for auld lang syne."*

ROSEDALE ABBEY - YORKSHIRE - ENGLAND

Rosedale Abbey Caravan Park was experiencing an unexpected glut of bookings.

Seven touring pitches and five glamping pods for a week apiece (members of a college field trip whose previous accommodation had become unavailable), seven tents for a varying number of nights, and one of their holiday cottages for a fortnight.

"Have the schools been given a surprise holiday?" asked the manager. "Thank goodness we finished the groundwork the other week, that's all I can say. When they arriving?"

"Field trip bus is due sometime after two and the rest? No idea."

The manager was present when the guests started to arrive, noticing that there were a number of unexpected caravans requesting a plot too.

However, just as she was about to make further enquires into the sudden popularity of her campsite, a member of staff approached at the run with the news that there was trouble in the lower cesspit and she forgot. There was nothing like raw sewage spilling out from a pipe to take your mind off pretty much everything else.

Meanwhile, in the privacy of their caravans, glamps and tents, the kerns were getting ready for the night's work.

In a holiday cottage in the village the Faie surveyors were pulling together their report.

They had spent the last week studying maps and geological surveys of the area, one having been prepared by the Faie a century before when there had been an investigation, alas not detailed enough, of the area around St Mary and St Church after a number of possible Kobold sightings.

"Found it," Aodh-Chi informed Raibert and Nansaidh after a glance at his sidekick Jockie. Jock was a full human, or Aonnan in the old tongue. He was Aodh's business partner and fully aware of his antecedents and of the Faie. The two and their equipment had arrived in Rosedale Abbey yesterday morning and had completed the study of the area under the pretext of doing a survey for the roads department.

That morning they had found what could only be the nunnery crypt, or at least an underground chamber of considerable size, which had probably been used as a crypt.

"There appears to be two entrances," said Jockie, pointing to the large-scale map open on the table. "One in the far corner of the churchyard beside the gate. Here. Easy enough to find and the other one by the stream."

"There are illusions in place but they're low strength," added Aodh. "I felt them immediately but Jockie here didn't. You can see right through them and hear through them. It's possible they get stronger if people get too close but I didn't get that impression, I certainly didn't feel them shifting."

"What's down there?' asked Raibert.

"Two large chambers, rock or stone, possibly manmade but could be natural," Jockie replied. "We'd have got more details if we'd been able to use the magnetometers but we did manage to detect clumps of metal."

"We could go back this evening," suggested Aodh. "With the magnometer and get information on exactly where you'll find metals, bricks, burning and the rock itself, perhaps even a plan."

Raibert shook his head regretfully.

"We don't want to warn them of our presence," he said. "Have you got any idea of the layout?"

"Two paths, tunnels really, and leading from the entrances. The metal deposits are there."

"That makes sense," said Nansaidh. "Weapons close to the entrance. That's where I would put them."

"Two chambers," continued Aodh.

"Right," said Raibert. "I don't think we should wait until tomorrow.

We'll go in tonight when it's dark. Jockie. You take Nansaidh to the entrance by the gate then come straight back here. I'll go with Aodh to the stream when you get back. Briefing at eighteen-hundred hours."

You could hear the silence.

The two groups of kerns could be seen only as shivers of movement by any passers-by but there weren't any out this late and in such dreadful weather.

It was cold, windy and wet, that smirry, blowy rain that soaked you through in minutes. The kerns were wearing wet weather camouflage gear but that didn't stop the dribbles, nor the puddles, those deep wallowing ones that every soldier hated.

Nansaidh sent Jockie back to the holiday cottage as soon as she sighted the gate.

She ordered half of her kerns to slip behind the churchyard wall and the others to melt into the copse beside the road.

Jockie sped back to where Raibert and the others were waiting beside the North Gill stream at the eastern side of the village, Raibert having decided that waiting at the caravan park was an invitation to be discovery by either an innocent passer by or a Kobold patrol who he was sure, would have heard about the recent off-peak visitors.

The muffle, Flidais's gift of concealment to her kindred, was be restricted to the area around the crypt and would settle as soon as Raibert and his kerns entered the shallow waters of the North Gill.

The Banduri who had accompanied the teams had been working on the illusion for hours, setting it slowly and quietly so as not to create an alarm.

Jockie passed them by with a jaunty wave and headed down the road towards the Coach House Inn, where Aodh was waiting. It was also the emergency rendezvous and where the buses and other vehicles were parked.

Raibert's earpiece bleeped. It was the Nansaidh's team at the other entrance to the crypt.

< No guards detected. We're going in. >

Raibert and his kerns slipped over the road and down into the stream, leaving four on guard, Kailen checking everyone's night visors and helmets as they took the plunge.

The stream was deeper than Raibert had expected. He gasped at the unexpectedness as the cold water hit his groin.

The entrance to the crypt wasn't large and it wasn't especially well hidden, but as Raibert remembered as he stooped under the lintel, it didn't need to be.

There were two types of hiding spells used by the Gods and Goddesses.

There was the one the Banduri of Goddess Flidais had set as soon as the last kern had entered the stream. It was known colloquially as a 'muffle'. It was usually short term, took a lot of energy, of which even gods possessed a finite amount, and was very powerful, masking all sound, sight and smell within.

It was used in battle situations, such as this one, used to hide what was happening from humankind, and protect them. Nothing would be able to pass through the barrier unless the Banduri, with the help of Flidais, opened a temporary door.

The other hiding spell was one of illusion, low energy and long term. Caisteal Na Sìobhragan was hidden using an illusion, as were a number of Faie dwellings and bastions in Scotland. The most important were hidden completely so that a person passing by could not see them. The illusion that covered Finlarig House, Raibert's home from home, was of the other kind, a lighter spell. It could be seen but no one ever paid it any attention, indeed, unless they were of the Faie, or attuned to the Faie, they would forget they had seen it almost as soon as they registered it as a building. Most 'out in the world' residences of the Faie and their friends had this type of protection.

Once inside the passage into the crypt, Raibert gagged. The smell of blood was overpowering and it wasn't the coppery scent of fresh either. He could see Hrolfr and Fionnuir wrapping a bandage from their medical packs round their noses and mouths, and Kailen was using his favourite bandana in an effort to stop himself from being sick. Along each side of the passage there were doors, some open, some shut.

The kerns were checking each one. Some, the empty ones, only took a minute or so, others took longer and others still, well, you wanted the check to only last seconds.

The Kobold have to have been here for years for the smell to be this bad, thought Raibert as he struggled on.

But if he thought the smell was bad now, it was nothing to the second when Fionnuir opened a large wooden door some yards further in.

What was inside was like the set of a horror film.

This'll be like what Caisteal Na Sìobhragan will become if Cailleach gets her way, thought Raibert with a shudder. Taking a deep breath, he took a closer look. There were human bodies in the room. The dead had a sweet, rancid and overripe smell that permeated skin and clothes. As he directed his torch towards the edge of the pile he spied the maggots that had made the pile of death resemble a huge singular monster that had emerged out of his worst nightmare. The pile was sitting in about three inches of body fluid. The liquid was moving.

"Shut the door," commanded Raibert as he backed away, before stopping and holding up his hand for silence.

There were sounds of fighting from Nansaidh's side of the crypt. Shots were being fired and he could hear the roar of the portable flamethrowers that intelligence had told him the Kobold had getting their hands on. Gunrunners would sell to anyone who had the money, including smelly, scary 'men' who smelt of stale blood.

As Raibert realised they were in for a really bloody battle in a place the enemy knew intimately and his kerns hardly at all, he felt air move on his cheek and turned … and just in time.

A dark figure leapt upon him. Raibert staggered on to one knee as he brought up his sword in an attempt to stop his enemy's down thrust. The pain as the blade sliced into his shoulder was every bit as bad as the pain he had experienced during his last encounter with a Kobold warrior but without the prickly, numbing sensation that meant this warrior hadn't coated his blade with poison.

He was bringing up his revolver to fire when there was a shot from his right and the Kobold gave a gasp and crumpled. There was another shot and his face became bleeding meat.

Raibert thanked Fionnuir with a nod as he got to his feet. "Careful everyone, approach each doorway with caution."

"You need a medic?" she asked.

"Just a scratch. My own fault, should have been keeping more of an eye out."

Then the screams hit and Raibert, completely forgetting his own advice, bounded along the corridor, his kerns at his heels and that was when they realised that the crypt was packed with hidden, and not so hidden, dangers.

When they were half way along the passage and the sounds of fighting getting louder, the floor gave way under Raibert and if it hadn't been for Hrolfr at his heels who, an instant later, bent and caught his belt; Raibert would have been a goner.

"This place will be full of booby traps," noted a worried Fionnuir who was keeping guard.

"Give me your hand," ordered Kailen.

"Aye, take mine too," added Hrolfr. "Come on Raibert."

Raibert managed to swing his body round enough and grasp Hrolfr's hand as tight as he could but fighting gloves weren't designed for dragging someone out of an abyss. Kailen managed to grab his other one and after that it wasn't long before the two kerns managed to pull him up.

"I owe you both a right right gude-willie waught for that," said a relieved Raibert, scrambling to his feet.

"More than one," Hrolfr grinned.

"It is a guid way doon," noted his brother. "I think a guidwull dram for me too."

It was a tradition, giving a goodwill drink for saving a life and both kerns had spent most of their lives in the north of Scotland where good manners and traditions were a part of life.

"Walk along the edges," advised Fionnuir who had been examining the trap. "There may be more."

They heard shouting and cheering from ahead and knew that Nansaidh and her kerns had bested the enemy.

They trooped along the passage, taking care to stand at the edge of the passage floor and reached the first crypt without any more incidents. Now they knew what they were looking for, the traps could be seen with the naked eye.

At the entrance, kerns were standing guard over two bodies.

"Eight Kobold killed," Tiobaid reported. "Three of us wounded. Making their own way to the medics."

The number of Kobold surprised Raibert. Eight was not a lot. "Where are the rest?" he asked.

"Nansaidh thinks there's a third passage. They're looking for it now in the big crypt through there. We've warned the outside guards."

"No prisoners?"

Tiobaid shook his head. "Those that were here, it was as if they had made a suicide pact."

"Ordered to delay us," Raibert surmised. "Death in battle would be better than refusing. Ovens are getting cold too," he added touching one, "they've been gone a few hours, probably saw us arriving at the caravan site, dammit."

And it was at this point that the call came through that they'd found the third passage, but after investigation it proved to be a dead end, literally.

It had caved in, crushing at least one Kobold to death. Noting that an exposed hand was clutching what looked like a briefcase handle, Raibert ordered the bodies excavated.

The briefcase contained a notebook, some maps and a glass vial containing blood.

Being careful not to break it, Raibert placed it back on top of the bodies before extracting the paperwork. He gave the maps and notebook to Nansaidh and as he searched for more.

Nansaidh opened the notebook. It was blank except for one page was filled with a crabbed, spidery script.

"Anyone read Latin?" she asked. "At least I think it's in Latin ... some of it."

"I do, a little," Raibert replied, holding out his hand. His childhood education had occurred during the Great War and the years that followed, he and his childhood friends had shared a classical education, normal for the time.

"Vaticinium," Raibert made out the words. "Latin for, I think, prediction, prophecy. Oraculum. Foribus oraculi. Oracle. Then a mix of Latin and Greek and my latter's worse than my former. It's been a long time. However, I'm pretty sure that word is Greek for a prophecy. We need to get this back to the researchers back at Caisteal Na Sìobhragan immediately."

"Are the Kobold working in response to a prophecy of some kind?" asked an incredulous Nansaidh.

"Surely not," said Fionnuir. "Why ... everyone knows they're not real. As my old teacher used to tell us, 'they have a habit of not happening'.

"Many people believe they often contain an element of truth," noted Raibert, putting the notebook away. "Right everyone, make sure there aren't any more little surprises lying around and someone, could you bind up this cut, it's nipping something awful."

It took the best part of the night to investigate the complex but at last the survey was complete. Élair and her sister Elaspeth found one last hidden chamber, a comfortable place with carpets on the floors topped by heavy old velvet covered furniture and damask bed drapes.

The two had given everyone a fright when they found a switch and pulled it. Every light in the place had come on. The light made investigating the nooks and crannies easier but did highlight some horrors the searchers would rather not have seen.

Fionnuir took photographs of a huge map of England affixed to one of the walls in a large alcove that resembled a military planning room and noted down the locations of all the little tags of various colours.

Nansaidh thought they might be Kobold bases but Raibert said they were more likely to be red herrings planted to put them off the scent. Despite all their precautions, the Kobold had known they were coming.

They did take a large wooden box full of trinkets, mostly jewellery and watches, the possessions of the uncounted victims over the years. Raibert thought the box might contain centuries of accumulated loot because a lot of the items looked very old.

"What now?" asked Hrolfr. "Block the entrances?"

Raibert shook his head. "An innocent might come across them by accident. We'll have to blow it. Did anyone remember to bring the dynamite?"

The muffle wouldn't 'muffle' the effects of the explosions completely so everyone would have to be back in their caravans, pods and cottage rooms when the entrances blew.

Hopefully it could be explained away as a natural tremor.

In ones, twos, threes and fours they slipped out of the crypt via the gate or stream until only three were left.

The dynamite was arranged and the explosion mechanisms set up.

Raibert gave the order to set the timers and the three left.

Once they were at the cottage he gave the word and the wireless detonator was activated.

From above ground, the effects of the explosion that destroyed the crypt were almost negligible, although the ground did shake a little bit. Some of the village dogs barked and there were some indignant remarks made by the cats but no one village human mentioned the explosion or the shaking the next morning.

Back at the campsite, the kerns went to bed, but not before they all made use of the shower blocks.

"Don't know about you but I'm going to get every stitch I'm wearing fumigated," said Hrolfr to his brother Kailen.

"I'm going to replace the grip on my sword hilt," noted Kailen. "Plus the fumigation, or perhaps a very hot fire."

"I'm throwing mine away and demanding a re-issue," agreed Fionnuir. "Tell me when you're about the put a match to that fire of yours."

"We'll be needing volunteers to go to the village store as soon as it's light to buy as much disinfectant, soap, and perfume they can get their hands on," noted Nansaidh.

"I've got cash in my room," offered Raibert.

"Goddess alive! Whatever cash you've got with you won't be enough!

I'm going to give them my bank card with permission to spend every last penny!"

The next day Raibert got in touch with a friend of his in the police, a very senior police officer.

Surveillance motorway cameras had picked up six large lorries with no company logos (and painted a plain army khaki green) travelling at speed west along the A170 then south on the M1 two hours before the kerns entered the crypt's passages.

When the trucks had reached the Birmingham area the vehicles had split up and disappeared off the motorways and into the lesser roads that did not have cameras.

Enquiries of the military led to the information that there had been no military convoys of that size on the road that night.

Bin-hix and his underlings had disappeared into thin air, free to wreck havoc another day.

CHAPTER 19

FLIDAIS

"Give thine ears, hear the words that are said, give thine heart to interpret them."

SOMEWHERE IN THE MILTIVERSE

Goddess Flidais had made a decision. The situation was serious. She asked for an audience with her father, the High God Jah.

Jah agreed, with the provision that all his children should be involved.

Out of the nine invited, six had accepted.

It was of no surprise to any god when Cailleach and Balar refused to attend, sending a snide little message to Flidais stating that they 'wouldn't be seen dead' in her company.

Flidais might have been forgiven for saying that their wish could be arranged but she didn't. Meirneal, the youngest god to accept the invitation, was not so forgiving and earned a reprimand from the God Lir. Lir was the eldest to attend the audience, the oldest brother, Ra, having declined.

This refusal had been anticipated. Ra took his duties as guardian of the First World really, really, really seriously and had only left it once during the last three million years. Flidais was exceedingly annoyed with her eldest brother, after all, they all lived in the one multiverse and she felt they were jointly and severally responsible for it. However, she kept her feelings to herself and she did love him.

The six, Lir, Nantosuelta, Herne, Aja, Flidais and Meirneal gathered around their father.

"Father, I have a boon to ask of you," said Flidais.

The all-knowing face turned to look at his middle daughter.

"I know of that what you wish," he said. "As you will know that I cannot accede to any one of your requests."

Flidais sighed.

"Give thy ears to listen, hear the words that I am saying, know in your heart why it must be so."

"I know Father but … I know what must be coming."

"I may know, but I think you do not know all that will transpire, and even I know not all of what must be. But I cannot permit access between the worlds for the Cuetiachtli. It would lead to chaos."

"Not any more chaos than if my sister brings all her Kobold and Balar's Spriggan through the vortexes to attack the world under my care."

"In this, my beloved daughter, you are wrong," Jah answered. "If I granted this boon the balance between worlds would be broken and a promise broken."

"What promise?"

"My promise to the mother of all, to keep the worlds separate and together, bound by her love. All love encompasses touch and distance, restraint and freedom but within the rules of life. So it is with us and we are bound."

"Rules? My people are dying!"

"As are mine," said Aja.

"And mine," said Herne.

"It must be so. Death is a part of life."

"And my other boon?" asked Flidais.

"You must continue to keep your distance," said Jah.

"But if I could just help them a little more?"

"You can let them know."

"Through the dreams?"

"They worked before."

"I believe my dear sister," said Nantosuelta, knowing the temper of Flidais of old, "that you can perhaps make your dreams more direct. I am sure Father will permit that."

"As long as they are not too much so," Jah agreed, "but no direct interference. And remember the law … 'Cha mharbh thu do bhràithrean agus do pheathraichean'. You must follow this rule, despite what they have done and might still do. Thou shalt not kill they brother or thy sister. You must bring them to me and I and I alone will punish."

"Yes Father." Flidais sighed. War was coming and she was not to be allowed to do anything to stop it.

"Many will die," she said. "Could you perhaps stop the connections between the worlds, at least for a while? That would stop her from bringing more soldiers to my world."

"That is not the answer," stated Aja. "We know Cailleach has warriors on both our worlds and also that of Herne. To cut the vortexes does not mean the war with Cailleach will not come, it would merely mean three separate, smaller wars."

"I agree," said Herne. "This way we can perhaps help each other … indirectly or course. We can share intelligence, help each other to find the strongholds of Cailleach and Balar."

"It's a pity she has the same amount of power as we do," added Flidais.

"That sharing of intelligence and indirect help is permitted," agreed Jah. "I wish I could do more, but you must remember that I am constrained by rules just as you are. My children, you have war and discord to contend with but so do I. Do not forget what I protect you all from."

"Father, I am sorry but all the creatures in my world are dear to me and I would save them," said Flidais.

"And I," said Lir.

"And I," said Nantosuelta.

"And I," said Herne.

"And I," said Aja.

"And I," said Meirneal.

"You don't have your world yet," said Lir.

"No I don't," said Meirneal. "Just wanted to demonstrate some solidarity."

This comment elicited a laugh and Jah took the opportunity to fade away.

"So all I'm left with is muffles and dreams," complained an unhappy Flidais. She had hoped this time, with the situation escalating; she might have got permission to help her Faie in the war against Cailleach.

Meirneal winked at her. She stopped feeling annoyed immediately.

One by one her brothers and sisters departed until only Meirneal remained. Flidais swung round at once.

"You have a plan. I know you have. Tell me."

"I need to work it out some more but I was thinking about our brother

Balar."

"What of him?"

"He is easily led. I was wondering if we, I, could tempt him away from Cailleach's less than benign influence."

"You would take on his governance?"

"I will."

"That would deal with the Spriggan. If we only had the Kobold to deal with …"

"I'll see what I can do. Now I must take my leave. Our Father likes company …"

He faded away without uttering another word. Meirneal had no world of his own … yet … so spent a lot of time with Father.

Flidais was left with a great many questions she would have liked to ask of him.

I do hope he's not biting off more than he can chew, she was thinking as she too faded away. Cailleach is formidable and ruthless. If she realises he's getting involved … but … perhaps Balar will remember old friendships and kindnesses. He and Meirneal were very close … once.

As Flidais floated through the void towards her world, old memories began to surface, memories about the days when she would walk the roads and glens of Scotland, taking hospitality and leaving good health and wellbeing in her wake.

Flidais remembered the bàrd singing by the fire, that night so long ago when she had first heard the song. It had been during the reign of Queen Mary, or perhaps it had been in the time of Mary's father King James the Fifth.

Those had been dangerous times for the Faie. Cailleach had tried to use the minority of the infant queen after her father's death in battle against the English to promote strife within the Kingdom of the Scots, this to further her plan to oust Flidais as Goddess and take her place.

Flidais had warned her Faie then, through dream songs, and they had got the point immediately, not using a version of *Auld Lang Syne* but another song, well known in that era, William Dunbar's *Sweit Rois of Vertew*.

Perhaps those researchers at Caisteal Na Sìobhragan who were overcomplicating things would make the connection if she replaced the song in the dreams with this earlier one, or … perhaps not. Perhaps she needed another song altogether.

Or … perhaps it was time for a change.

Perhaps she should disobey her father and employ a more hands-on approach.

HOLOCENE WORLD

Once Flidais reached her world, she stopped and watched it spin round once on its axis and after some thought, decided that everything happening on it was within manageable proportions.

True, humanity was engaged in all sorts of activities, some were nefarious, some were destructive but it was, on the whole, not doing enough to bring down her wrath, at least not at this time.

She checked the vortexes, her supernatural senses attuned to what was happening within. There were no large numbers of Kobold or Spriggan moving between the worlds at the behest of her sister Cailleach.

Once she was satisfied there was not any immediate danger, she checked in on a number of individuals destined, because of their blood kin, to take part in the most important mission in the history of the Multiverse. In fact, the continuance of the Multiverse itself might depend on their success.

She first looked at those who were living in Britannica, England first.

She began with Vero and two members of his family. Much to her satisfaction, she discovered that the family's arrangements to visit Vero's eldest son were progressing nicely.

Her spirit self then floated north towards Milton Keynes. Sosaidh and Eoin were alive and well. They could stay right where they were in the meantime. Protection was in place. They should be safe enough.

She visited Leicester next, to check in on how another of her charges was getting on. Things were progressing nicely there too. She must remember to remind the young lady in a dream of warning not to try and wriggle out of attending the trip.

She floated north into Scotland and looked in on Vero's eldest in his flat in Perth's city centre.

On a whim, she swooped in on Finlarig House but Raibert wasn't there, so she travelled further north to Caisteal Na Sìobhragan to check in on the youngest. He appeared happy and content, which was a good thing. Flidais loved children. She was unhappy about the fact that he soon might have to perform tasks that would frighten the bravest adult, never mind a ten-year-old. Let him have his fun.

She sped over the Atlantic towards the United States of America. Yes. All was well there and she had already asked her brother Herne about the two last. They were alive and he would keep an eye on them.

Flidais was relieved. She had located eleven. Eleven was the number. It was however the minimum number. She couldn't afford to lose any more.

She could feel it in her bones. It would soon be time to tell him the truth. They would all know the truth about the future.

She decided to leave her hunt for the one that was still missing until another time.

CHAPTER 20

FIELD TRIP

"For auld lang syne, my jo, for auld lang syne,
We'll tak' a cup o' kindness yet, for auld lang syne."

LEICESTER - LEICESTERSHIRE - ENGLAND

Amelia Bunty woke with a start. The nightmare had returned. She was being chased by a huge, slavering wraith in female form with teeth that were so long it was a wonder the creature could open her mouth. Amelia always woke up before she found out what the wraith was trying to stop her from doing. It was all very frustrating.

There was also the problem of the singing woman invading her dreams ever other night… "For auld lang syne, my jo, for auld lang syne …"

Amelia looked over at her alarm clock and for the second time that week and the fourth time this month, realised she was going to be late for her geology lecture.

Dr Pratt would be annoyed *again*.

Dr Pratt was the absolute master of the sarcastic word. Sadly, he didn't appear to realise that sarcasm was the lowest form of wit. She got up, took a quick shower and put on some clean clothes without checking if everything matched. She decided she didn't have time for breakfast. As she gathered up her laptop and thrust it into her holdall, Amelia wondered what acidic comments she would have to suffer today.

"Amelia Bunty!"
Amelia looked up.

"Your classmates would appreciate it if you would at least *try* to pay attention?"

Amelia's eyes snapped open and focused on Dr Pratt. He was shaking his head with un-amused exasperation.

"Of all my students," he thundered. "You have been the most inattentive." The words echoed inside Amelia's head. How often had she listened to this complaint? Fact was, she didn't like this class and wished she'd chosen something else for her third subject at the beginning of the academic year.

She looked down.

"Amelia Bunty! Look at me! What have I been talking about?"

Amelia's mind was a blank. What *had* he been talking about? What was the topic for today? She hated these subsidiary lectures in the small classrooms. You couldn't hide at the back so Dr Pratt was able to see exactly who was paying attention and who was not.

Dr Pratt's eyes were flashing dangerously. Amelia groaned. She looked round at the nineteen other students in an attempt to get a hint but they were all staring at Dr Pratt, all that is but the small weedy looking guy opposite. He winked and clenching his hands made an up and down motion as if he was driving. She hadn't a clue what he was trying to tell her.

She might not know the answer to the question but she did know she was in deep trouble … again.

She looked down at the pad of paper on her desk. Unfortunately it wasn't any help because it was as blank now as it had been at the beginning and it was … she took a surreptitious look at her watch, now ten to the hour.

"You wish to pass this course?" asked Dr Pratt in the most sarcastic voice he could muster.

"Yes Dr Pratt. I *do* wish to pass."

The thought of spending a repeat year under the tutelage of Dr Pratt filled her with dread, and then there was the problem of finding the fees and the wherewithal to live if she did have to repeat. Passing two foundation classes in another science (there was a list to choose from) was a prerequisite to obtaining her degree in environmental geography. Foundation Geology was the second of her choices.

"So what have I been talking about?"

"Er, plate tectonics?" she hazarded.

"That was the subject of last week's lecture," he snapped. "Get the notes for today from one of your classmates and copy them out. And you'll do well to remember that this trip is obligatory. Passing your exams and assignments is not enough. No field trip means you fail the entire course and you'll have to repeat it next year."

She nodded vigorously, realising that he must have been talking about the field trip and why weedy Lucien had been pretending to drive.

"Right," said Dr Pratt, turning to the whiteboard. "Everyone take this down."

Amelia looked at the whiteboard, picked up her pen and began to write, wishing Dr Pratt would permit computers in his classroom. He was quite impossibly old-fashioned. He would declare to everyone who would listen (and those who could not get away fast enough) that he had always taught this way and that it was working very well, thank you very much.

As she wrote, Amelia absently pondered about how the head of the geology department had managed to persuade him to issue abbreviated lecture notes at the end of each class. *Probably threatened him with dismissal*, she thought as she wrote, her biro digging into the paper so hard it tore.

She wrote it all down, word for word, just in case he decided to check. She wouldn't put it past him.

Saturday. Ten o'clock. Bus will leave from the parking bay in front of this building. Do not be late or it will leave without you and you will fail the course.

She suspected he had added that bit specifically for her.

"Equipment list," Dr Pratt said, waving a small bundle of paper. He was waving so hard some sheets fluttered to the ground. He didn't bother picking them up. "Get hold of one on the way out. Don't leave anything behind, the cottage we've rented is a long way from the nearest shop so if you forget anything you'll have to do without it for the entire fortnight."

Amelia groaned. She liked her home comforts. A cottage in the Highlands squeezed into a tiny room with people she didn't know. And no shops! This sounded like purgatory of the most devilish kind. It probably didn't have electric light! No electricity at all! No showers! Amelia didn't know a lot about country living.

"Don't forget to bring sandwiches," added Dr Pratt. "The journey to Kinlochbervie takes around six hours."

Amelia groaned again. Sandwiches. *There's probably not a motorway café anywhere on the way there,* she thought. *Probably no motorways!* Amelia knew even less about the road systems in Scotland than she did about living in the country. She looked down at her manicured nails and sighed.

This field trip was a nuisance. She hadn't known about it when she had chosen to take foundation geology instead of chemistry. As a matter of fact, if she were honest with herself, she would have to admit that she hadn't read through the detailed course description before ticking the selection box. The only person she could blame was her own sweet self. She couldn't fail the course and have to repeat (including the awful field trip) next session in addition to the three courses she would be taking as part of her geography degree.

However, there were better ways to spend the first two weeks of your time between exams and the summer vacation.

Amelia might not have been late for the bus but she was no more reconciled to the field trip than she had been at the beginning of the week. Much to her annoyance, the most voluble students on the course slipped into the seat beside her and began to talk from the moment he sat down.

It was Lucien. As he was the only one to have attempted to get her out of trouble with Dr Pratt earlier in the week, she smiled and decided to make the best of it.

"Aren't you excited to be going to the Lewisian Gneiss Complex at last? I am. I've been looking forward to the trip all term," he said.

Forcing a smile, Amelia said that she wasn't entirely sure what a Lewisian Gneiss Complex was.

He wondered aloud how she had managed to get through the course without this particular item of knowledge.

"I concentrated on the rocks of later periods for the exam," she answered. She had crammed day and night during that week before the exam. "Carboniferous period in the central belt and also plate tectonics," she added.

Amelia might be lazy regarding her geology studies but she wasn't stupid. An investigation of past papers had informed her that these two subjects *always* came up and in a two question-answer exam that was all she needed to know about to attain the pass mark.

"The contribution of the northwest Scottish Highlands to our understanding of tectonic processes is immense," he agreed.

"Really?"

"Some of the rocks are over 3,000 million years old!"

"Fascinating," Amelia commented in a voice calculated to put an end to this particular conversation before it arrived at a place that would expose the full extent of her ignorance. It didn't work.

"And we're going on an expedition to the mountain known as Foinaven!" he added with so much enthusiasm that the contents of his cola can fizzled up and spilled over on to his knees. Lucien didn't notice.

"You've spilt your juice," Amelia informed him.

After a perfunctory mopping up, Lucien continued to talk and his captive audience perforce, had to listen. She caught some sympathetic looks from the pair sitting across the aisle but they made no attempt to intervene. Amelia felt rather resentful about the situation but it had to be said that Amelia learned a lot about Pre-Cambrian rock formations in the six hours that followed.

That evening, as they ate their evening meal, Lucien sat beside her. He remained at her side the whole evening

It was with a great deal of relief that she lay down in her bunk that night, and she was asleep in minutes. Lucien Lalage was a most exhausting companion!

NEAR KINLOCHBERVIE - SUTHERLAND - SCOTLAND

Amelia had always believed she was as fit as the next person. She attended a keep fit class twice a week, but that first day proved she wasn't as physically prepared as she thought.

Before the field trip, Amelia, a city girl, had believed walks and climbs in mountain areas were easy. She had imagined wandering along peaceful, paved (if not paved at least well defined and trodden) paths, scrambling up and down through woods of well-tended pine trees, and catching the occasional glimpse of a golden crested eagle or a cheeky little squirrel.

Wrong.

During the first day's walk, although she wouldn't admit it to anyone, especially Lucien, her heart had pounded so hard she thought it would burst. She had felt it through her heart and eyes; *bump, bump, bump*; and that wasn't all. She felt every muscle screaming at the unaccustomed exercise and the feeling was more agonising than she was prepared to admit.

She kept going. There was no way she was going to admit defeat, especially in front of Lucien with his alabaster skin and sticklike legs. He was proving to be an experienced hill walker. *She* had to stop and catch her breath every few hundred yards or so, and accepting as truth Dr Pratt's advice of 'on no account sit down or straining muscles might seize'.

They seized eleven times in the first day alone.

Lucien, dropping back to walk and rest with her, advised that she should, instead of thinking about how far they had to go, break the walk into little pieces and walk a mile at a time, focusing on certain things ahead like individual trees and boulders. It helped, and she began to appreciate the value of Lucien's company, at least a little more than she had until then.

When they reached their first geological examination site, a rock formation about 700 feet above sea level she felt a sense of deep accomplishment and despite her aching legs set to with the hammer at her designated spot with an enthusiasm she hadn't known she possessed. At least she was sitting down.

That night she slept like a log after the liberal use of the embrocation salve provided by Dr Pratt.

The second day was not as bad as the first and the third easier than the second.

Their third expedition was to a granite intrusion that had formed during the geological era known as the early Devonian.

"It's absolutely amazing that these rocks were formed four hundred million years ago," observed Lucien as he carefully chipped away at a piece of granite set within an earlier metamorphic rock-bed.

"What's that other rock called?" Amelia asked. She and Lucien had been paired off again. She didn't entirely appreciate Dr Pratt's decision; she found Lucien's earnest approach to the subject somewhat of a trial but that morning, as she watched him work she decided he wasn't so bad after all. He did know a lot about geology and had been helping her a lot, especially with their nightly reports.

"Archaen gneiss."

"How old is that?"

Lucien squinted at her.

"Did you attend *any* of the first term lectures?"

"Some."

He shook his head.

"Three thousand nine hundred to three thousand six hundred million years ago."

Amelia blinked.

"Goodness! That's a long time! How was it formed?"

"Read about it," he said, concentrating on his rock hammer manipulation. "Like the rest of us do. Ah ..."

He removed a small piece of rock and began to examine it through his hand lens. He glanced at Amelia. She looked a bit downcast and he felt sorry for her.

"You got your bit?" he asked.

She shook her head. She was sucking her finger. Amelia wasn't an expert with a hammer.

"Take mine," he said, placing his own sample into her hand. "I can get another."

"Only if you show me where I can learn about this archaen gneiss stuff," she grinned as she accepted the sample.

So far, the field trip had gone as well as foundation level field trips always did.

The majority of the participants were interested in what they were investigating, a few were intense in their enthusiasm, Lucien Lalage included, and a few were, quite frankly, bored. Half way through the trip, to Amelia's surprise, Dr Pratt included her name as a member of the larger, middle group. He had been surprised too.

It was more fun examining and touching the rocks than reading about them or looking at pictures. She began to wonder if she might be able to take geology as a subject next year.

On the penultimate day, Dr Pratt took a group of twelve students on an expedition up the mountain known as Foinaven, situated about ten miles east of Kinlochbervie. Today's expedition was what Amelia called, the 'extra-voluntary' part of the field trip. Dr Pratt had been surprised and pleased when eleven undergraduate students appeared at the breakfast table, the others having elected to have a lie in. The eleven made sandwiches for the day ahead, suffered Dr Pratt and the graduate student's scrutiny of their clothing and equipment in good part, and departed at eight o'clock sharp.

By this time Amelia was finding the walks to their sample sites, if not easy, at least bearable.

They reached Foinaven's summit and began setting up the windbreakers and the temporary camp. Amelia and Lucien elected to sit behind some rock slabs. They were a more effective shelter than the breakers. There was a slight depression in the ground they could both squeeze inside if they were careful where they put their feet.

It was noon and they were tucking into their lunch with enthusiastic appetites. The views from the summit were breath taking.

"You can identify some of the Moine Thrust outcrops from here," said a thrilled Lucien in a loud excited voice, enthusiastically throwing part of his egg sandwich into the wind.

Amelia laughed.

Lucien's personality was growing on her. He would never be boyfriend material, but a sincere friendship was developing. She did recognise one thing. He was much cleverer than she was.

He'll probably end up as a famous geologist, she thought at least once a day.

The sun was warm and although it was windy, Amelia and Lucien were sitting inside the depression behind the slabs so they didn't feel it. They could hear the others' voices. They came and went depending on the wind direction.

I could lie down and have a rest, thought Amelia. She leant back in a semi prone position, her hands behind her head.

Lucien followed suit.

They dozed.

They didn't notice the mist that crept over their bodies inch by inch.

The mist was so thick sound could not penetrate.

They didn't hear Dr Pratt and the others calling their names.

It was the stillness that alerted Lucien, that and a sense of a creeping coldness.

They put on their thick jackets and safety belts then tried to work out where the others were.

They couldn't.

They didn't hear Dr Pratt's dismay when he couldn't get his mobile to work or the others exclaiming at the same phenomenon. For some reason they never thought about trying to use theirs.

Dr Pratt's voice became frantic. The others began blowing their whistles.

Lucien and Amelia didn't hear a thing. They grabbed their rucksacks and took each other's hand as they had been taught. Lucien's hands shook as he clipped the mountaineering ropes to the carabiner clips on their belts so they would not get separated.

They did not know that Dr Pratt and the others had begun their descent from the summit.

Dr Pratt knew the changeable nature of the weather here. He knew that Lucien and Amelia were carrying foul weather gear in their rucksacks. He had checked himself. He had supervised their mountain training the first day of the field trip. Lucien knew exactly what to do and Amelia was sensible. She would do what Lucien told her to do.

Although he was worried, Dr Pratt was positive the two were not in a life-threatening situation. He would get in touch with mountain rescue and fully expected that once the mist had evaporated the duo would be found.

They were half way down the mountain when the wind and rain hit.

Amelia and Lucien held on tightly to each other in an effort to stay on their feet.

"I'll get the flare out," Lucien shouted but the words were swept away. He dropped one of her hands.

"No …" she screamed.

The wind, instead of blowing against them began to swirl around them.

Amelia's feet left the ground. There was a strange ringing in her ears.

She lost her grip of Lucien's other hand.

It was like dropping from an aeroplane at night with no parachute.

Amelia's body was being buffeted like a rag doll and there was nothing she could do about it. The pain was excruciating and she felt certain that after all the bones in her body were broken, she would die.

She welcomed unconsciousness like an old friend. Anything was better than the pain of the buffeting wind within the vortex.

The story continues in Faie Castle (Caisteal Na Sìobhragan).

CHARACTERS & APPENDICES

1. THE GODS

JAH - God of All. He is the Father of the Nine Gods.

RA - He is the God of the First World, the Proterozoic. In the history of our world Ra was the Ancient Egyptian God of the sun. (Cuetiachtli - Druas.)

LIR - He is the God of the Second World, the Silurian. In the history of our world Lir is/was the Celtic God of the sea. (Cuetiachtli - Sidhe.)

NANTOSUELTA - She is the Goddess of the Third World, the Permian. In the history of our world Nantosuelta is/was the Celtic Goddess of fire, nature, fertility, rivers and the earth. (Cuetiachtli - Siofra.)

HERNE - He is the God of the Fourth World the Cretaceous. In the history of our world Herne was the Germanic God of forests and wild animals. (Cuetiachtli - Fladhaich.)

AJA - He is the God of the Fifth World, the Pleistocene. In the history of our world Aja is/was the African God of the forest and the animals within it. (Cuetiachtli - Ljosalfar.)

FLIDAIS - She is the Goddess of the Sixth World. In the history of our world Flidais is/was the Celtic Goddess of forest, woodland and wild things. This is our world, Earth, which we, the readers of this series, live in today. (Cuetiachtli - Faie.)

MEIRNEAL - He is the Future God of the Seventh World. In the history of our world Meirneal was the God of Magic. He is known as Merlin in England, Meirneal in Scotland, Myrddin in Wales, and Meirluin in Ireland. He has not yet revealed himself as a god in corporeal form but has been known in the past to have come to the aid of his brothers and sisters. (Cuetiachtli - unknown.)

CAILLEACH - She is the Goddess with no world. In the history of our world Cailleach is/was the Celtic Goddess of disease and plague and known as the veiled one. (Cuetiachtli - Kobold.)

BALAR - He is the God with no world. In the history of our world Balar is/was the Celtic God of drought and blight. (Cuetiachtli - Spriggan.)

2. NA COÌG LAGHAN AN DIA ÀRD

(THE FIVE LAWS OF THE HIGH GOD JAH)

1. CHIAD LACH
Cruthachadh tha Trì
(Creation is Three)
2. AN DÀRNA LACH
Cha mharbh thu do bhràithrean agus do pheathraichean.
(Thou shalt not kill thy brothers and thy sisters.)
3. TREAS LAGH
Tha sìth trì.
 (Peace is three.)
4. AN CEATHRAMH LACH
Bidh clann agus òigridh air an dìon agus air am meas airson an àm ri teachd.
 (Children and youth wilt be protected and cherished for they art the future.)
5. AN COÌGEAMH LAGH
Trì de na sìth Bidh buadhachadh.
 (Three of the peace wilt prevail.)

3. THE PARALLEL WORLDS

In our world, the multiverse is a hypothetical phenomena, defined as a group of multiple universes that include the one in which we exist.

The World of the God Ra - The First World - The Proterozoic World - The Time of the Air. This world began at the point when oxygen appeared on Planet Earth (c. 2,500 m.y.a).

The World of the God Lir - The Second World - The Silurian World - The Time of the Water. This world began at the time of the extinction level event at the end of the Precambrian Proterozoic period on Planet Earth (c. 542 m.y.a).

The World of the Goddess Nantosuelta - The Third World - The Permian World - The Time of the Supercontinent. This world began at the time of the extinction level event at the end of the Silurian period on Planet Earth (c. 416 m.y.a).

The World of the God Herne - The Fourth World - The Cretaceous World - The Time of the Dinosaurs. This world began at the time of the extinction level event at the end of the Permian period on Planet Earth (c. 251 m.y.a).

The World of the God Aja - The Fifth World - The Pleistocene World - The Time of the Ice. This world began at the time of the extinction level event at the end of the Cretaceous period on Planet Earth (c. 65.5 m.y.a).

The World of the Goddess Flidais - The Sixth World - The Holocene World - The Time of Man. This world began at the time of the extinction level event at the end of the Pleistocene period on Planet Earth (c. 11,700 y.a). This is the world we live in today.

The World of the God Meirneal - The Seventh World. This world exists only in the mind of the High God Jah.

4. THE KINDRED

The Cuetiachtli are the Children of the Gods. The details about their origins are lost in the depths of time but they are mortal beings created by the High God Jah to aid his god-children (Ra, Lir, Nantosuelta, Herne, Aja, Flidais, Meirneal, Cailleach and Balar) with their tasks. Each kindred group is given a new name when a new parallel world is formed when half of the kindred are left behind in the old world and the other half advance to the new world.

The exceptions to this rule are the Kobold and the Spriggan.

The Druas - First World.
The Sidhe - Second World.
The Siofra - Third World.
The Fladhaich - Fourth World.
The Ljosalfar - Fifth World.
The Faie - Sixth World.
The Jinni - Seventh World Cuetiachtli do not yet exist.
The Kobold - The kindred belonging to Goddess Cailleach. Female Kobold are known as Kobolda.

The Spriggan - The kindred belonging to God Balar.

The Kindred of Cailleach and Balar are not always recognised as such.

5. THE RACES

Aonnan - Homo sapiens. Us. Humans as we know them today. The Aonnan live in the World of the Goddess Flidais, The Sixth World, Planet Earth, in the here and now. Although technically, the designation Aonnan means every human, in practical terms it has come to mean all humans linked to the Faie and working with the Faie to protect the planet.

Bloden - The Bloden come from the Fourth World, the Cretaceous World. The Bloden are the descendants of the Cuetiachtli kindred the Fladhaich and a now extinct reptilian creature (a dinosaur) called a Troodon. Confusingly, the evolved descendants of the Troodons are also called Troodons. Their eyes are a very pale blue. It is now difficult to tell the difference between a pure bred Fladhaich and a Bloden unless they are eating. As they have both Cuetiachtli and earth-blood in their veins they can travel between the parallel worlds.

Daonna - The Daonna come from the Sixth World, the Holocene World. The Daonna are the descendants of the Cuetiachtli kindred the Faie and homo sapiens. Their eyes are predominately green. As they have both Cuetiachtli and earth-blood in their veins they can travel between the parallel worlds.

Guem - The Guem come from the Fifth World, the Pleistocene World. The Guem are the descendants of the Cuetiachtli kindred the Ljosalfar and Neanderthal humans. Their eyes are yellow with a brown or black pupil. As they have both Cuetiachtli and earth-blood in their veins they can travel between the parallel worlds.

Kobold - They are direct descendants of purebred Cuetiachtli adapted by Goddess Cailleach but can also travel between the parallel worlds. It is not known how Goddess Cailleach adapted those unfortunates to allow them to do so. They are very intelligent and efficient, cold-blooded fighters. They bear a superficial resemblance to the Bloden but no one who knows the Bloden would be fooled for long. Their eyes are black with white irises.

Spriggan - They are direct descendants of purebred Cuetiachtli adapted by Goddess Cailleach but can also travel between the parallel worlds. It is not known how God Balar adapted those unfortunates to allow them to do so (but he probably with Cailleach's help). They are not very intelligent; nor are they the most efficient at fighting. They have a hairy body but it is not as hirsute as furry mammals such as dogs and bears. Their eyes are black with white irises.

6. THE CHARACTERS

THE CUETIACHTLI - FAIE - Origin - The Sixth World (Holocene) - Alba (Scotland)

Aed Mac Searc Gwrtheyrn Mael - Aed-Chi. Fourth child, third son of Searc Mael. Ri-Beag after death of Torean. Later Àrd-Righ (High King) of the Faie of the Sixth World. Father of Kiah Mac Aed Mael. He is a widower. His beloved wife died when Kiah was born.

Aksel Mac Siosal Dubh - Aksel-Chi. A boy-child at Caisteal Na Sìobhragan. Age 10.

Andaer Mac Aodghan Bruis - Andaer-Chi. Tutor to Aed Mael, Raibert, Caoimhe and Nimue. He is the father of Andaerean-Chi.

Andaerean Mac Andaer Bruis - Andaerean-Chi. His father, Andaer Mac Aodghan Bruis, was tutor to amongst others, Raibert and Aed Mael. Andaerean is the leader of the team in Leicestershire, England where he works as a school headmaster. He uses the pseudonym Mr Bruce Anderson.

Aodh - Aodh-Chi. Surveyor who runs a surveying business outside Edinburgh. Business partner is Jockie.

Caoimhe Eibhlín Ní Domhnaill - Caoimhe-Chi. Daughter of an influential Irish Faie.

Ceiteig - Ceiteig-Chi. Nanny to the Frisealach family.

Concobhar MacGabhann - Concobhar-Chi. A kern (warrior).

Daidh Mac Padair Siosal - Daidh-Chi. Senior member of the Faie Security Team at Caisteal Na Sìobhragan.

Dalach Mac Buiseif Oig - Dalach-Chi. Faie academic. In charge of the research and development department and the vortex links to geological formations through the ages. Based at Caisteal Na Sìobhragan.

Eanruig Mac Searc Mael - First child, oldest son and heir of Searc Mael. Ri-Beag.

Élair Nic Abioy Chombaich - Élair-Chi. A warrior. Elder sister of Elaspeth. Younger sister of Giol.

Elaspeth Nic Abioy Chombaich - Elaspeth-Chi. A trainee kern (warrior). Younger sister of Élair. Younger sister of Giol.

Elsbeth Nic Searc Mael - Third child, oldest daughter of Searc Mael.

Fionn Mac na Maoile - Fionn-Chi. He uses the pseudonym Finn

MacMillan when operating in the human world where he works as an Inspector. Police Scotland, OSU (Operational Support Unit).

Fionnuir Nic Sosaidh Arasgain - Fionnuir-Chi. A kern (warrior).

Gaisgeil-Chi - Kern in the service of Nimue's family.

Giol Mac Aboiy Chombaich - Giol-Chi. A kern (warrior). Fionaven Mountain and Vortex Guard. Elder brother of Élair and Elaspeth.

Hrolfr Mac Uarraig Griogalach - Hrolfr-Chi. A kern (warrior). Brother of Kailen.

Kailen Mac Uarraig Griogalach - Kailen-Chi. A kern (warrior). Brother of Hrolfr.

Kiah Mac Aed Mael - Kiah-Chi. Ri-Beag (Under King) of the Faie of the Sixth World. Son of Aed Mac Gwrtheyrn Mael. He is presently attached to the American Faie.

Marsail Nic Dughlas Blar - Marsail-Chi. In overall command of the Faie Security Team in Scotland.

Moireach Nic Searc Mael - Fifth child, youngest daughter of Searc Mael.

Nansaidh Nic Ellair Druimeineach - Nansaidh-Chi. Fo Ceannard (Sub Commander) of the Army of the Faie in Alba.

Nimue Nic Giol Blàr - Nimue-Chi. She is the daughter of a prominent Scottish Faie and childhood friend of Aed Mael and Raibert.

Orlagh-Chi - Faie academic. A member of the research and development department at Caisteal Na Sìobhragan. She has an undergraduate degree in Scottish Literature from the University of Edinburgh.

Raibert Mac Prainnseas Frisealach - Raibert-Chi. Later, Ceannard (Commander) of the Army of the Faie of Alba. He uses the pseudonym Robert MacFraser when operating in the human world.

Searc Mael - King (Ard Righ) of the Faie and father of Aed Mael.

Sineag - Sineag-Chi. A girl-child at Caisteal Na Sìobhragan. Age 12.

Tiobaid Mac Dughlas Blar - Tiobaid-Chi. Warrior-kern and later a member of the Faie Security Team.

Torean Mac Searc Mael - Second child, second son of Searc Mael. Ri-Beag after death of Eanruig.

Torian-Chi - Faie academic. A member of the research and development department. He has a postgraduate degree in Scottish Literature from the University of Glasgow. The topic of his degree had centred around the poet Robert Burns. Based at Caisteal Na Sìobhragan.

Zellair Mac Solamh Paorach - Zellair-Chi. Fechtmesiter (Weaponsmaster) of the Faie.

THE CUETIACHTLI - FAIE - Origin - The Sixth World (Holocene) - Wind River Range (America)

Accalia - Accalia-Chi. Legionary. Tesserarius Mato's Centum X. 6th Contubernium. Friend of Liciana. Her surname is Moch.

Caso - Caso-Chi. Legionary. Tesserarius Mato's Centum X. 6th Contubernium. Brother of Chanti.

Chanti - Chanti-Chi. Legionary. Tesserarius Mato's Centum X. 6th Contubernium. Brother of Caso.

Liciana - Liciana-Chi. Legionary Tesserarius Mato's Centum X. 6th Contubernium. Friend of Accalia. Deceased.

Mato - Mato-Chi. Tesserarius. Commanding officer of Centum X in the Army of the Faie in the Americas.

Paavo - Paavo-Chi. Legionary. An experienced soldier of Tesserarius Mato's Centum X. 6th Contubernium.

Thelonius - Thelonius-Chi. Legionary. An experienced soldier of Tesserarius Mato's Centum X. 6th Contubernium.

Viho - Viho-Chi. Praeceptolem (Army Commander) of the Army of the Faie in the Americas.

THE GUEM - Origin - The Fifth World (Pleistocene)

Ahtna of the Manktire Clan - Part of the team in Leicestershire, England. She works as a mathematics teacher.

THE DAONNA - Origin - The Sixth World (Holocene)

Amelia Bunty - Foundation Year Geology student.

Aven - Daona academic. A member of the research and development department. He has an undergraduate degree in Scottish History from the University of St Andrews. Based at Caisteal Na Sìobhragan.

Hamilton Wayman - Palaeontology graduate in the employ of the Faie. Age 26.

Harold Wayman - A Professor of Archaeology. He was born and brought up in the world of humankind after his parents decided it was not safe for him to remain as a part of the World of Faie. His real name is Varo Mac Lobhdain Moch. His mother was called Aislinn.

John Gillycuddy - Eoin Mac Giolla Mochuda. Brother of Susan/Sosaidh. Son of Angela/Aingealog.

Lucien Lalage - Foundation Year Geology student.

Susan Gillycuddy - Sosaidh Nic Giolla Mochuda. Sister of John/Eoin. Daughter of Angela/Aingealog Gillycuddy.

THE AONNAN - Origin - The Sixth World (Holocene)

Aislinn (Alison) Wayfleet - Mother of Harold.

Alexander Gillycuddy - Stepfather of Susan/Sosaidh and John/Eoin. He is a builder by trade.

Angela Gillycuddy - Aingealog Nic Ahearn Bochanan - Mother of Susan/Sosaidh and John/Eoin. She spent most of her first marriage at Caisteal Na Sìobhragan but rejected the life on the death of her first husband when with her daughter and son, she left to live in the world with humankind when she met and married Alexander Gillycuddy.

Ethan - A homeless teenager.

Jamie Strachan - Sergeant. Police Scotland, OSU (Operational Support Unit).

Jockie - Surveyor who runs a surveying business outside Edinburgh. Business partner is Aodh-Chi.

Nanny Riddel - Nanny to the family Nanny Ceiteig worked for when she was young.

Oliver - A homeless teenager.

Phoebe - A homeless teenager.

Tristram Pratt - Geology professor. Known as Dr Pratt.

THE KOBOLD

Ahn-ran-hix - One of Goddess Cailleach's sub-commanders (a zapovjednik). Vin-ran-olt-hix's second-in-command.

Bin-hix - One of Goddess Cailleach's sub-commanders (a zapovjednik).

Id-hix - One of Goddess Cailleach's junior sub-commanders (a zapovjednik).

San-hix - One of Goddess Cailleach's sub-commanders (a zapovjednik).

Vin-ran-olt-hix - Goddess Cailleach's senior zapovjednik. Commander-in-Chief of All the Armies of Cailleach.

Zen-hix - One of Goddess Cailleach's sub-commanders (a zapovjednik).

7. THE PLACES

Alba - The Scottish Gaelic name for Scotland. There are parallels with Irish Gaelic Albann/Albainn, Manx Nalbin, Cornish Brythonic Alban and Welsh Brythonic Yr Alban. The third Brythonic language, Breton's word for Scotland is Bro-Skos (country of the Scots) but used in times past to mean Britain as a whole.

Banstead Village - Village in Surrey, England, 13 miles south of Central London. It was first recorded Anglo-Saxon charter in 987.

Beck Hole - Small historic village in North York Moors National Park, seventeen miles north east of Pickering, England.

Bedford - A county town in Bedfordshire, England.

Caisteal Na Sìobhragan - Faie Castle. Headquarters and control hub of the Faie in Scotland and in overall charge of everywhere else in the world. Seat of the High King of the Faie. It is situated somewhere in Sutherland, north of Foinaven Mountain, Scotland. (Sixth World.)

Castle Crah (Caisteal Creig) - A hill in the N-W part of the Fells in the Lake District, England.

Chaill Iolaire Stùc - The Cuetiachtli Training School in the Americas. The Sixth World. Translated, Chaill Iolaire Stùc means Lost Eagle Peak. It is situated somewhere in Wyoming.

Coombe Bissett - Village in Wiltshire, England southwest of Salisbury.

Craigdarroch is the name of a house, Dumfries and Galloway, Scotland. Once the seat of the Chief of the Fergussons of Dumfriesshire.

Cropton - A village and civil parish in the Ryedale district of North Yorkshire, England.

Cumnock - (Cumnag -Scottish Gaelic). A town in Ayrshire, Scotland.

Dablingneachd - The Stronghold of Goddess Cailleach and the Kobold. (Fifth World.)

Daingneachd - The Stronghold of Goddess Cailleach and the Kobold. It is situated somewhere in the west of Scotland. (Sixth World.)

Dervel (Darvel - Dairvel - Darbhail) - Small town in Irvine Valley, Ayrshire, Scotland, called the 'Lang Toon' and adjoins the village or Priestland.

Dibden - Village in Hampshire, England, dating from Middle Ages. In a valley at Eastern edge of the New Forest that runs into Southampton Water.

Drumclog - A small village in Lanarkshire, Scotland. Site of the Battle of Dumclog, 1679.

Dùnfuil - The Stronghold of Goddess Cailleach and the Kobold. (Fourth World.) Dùn fuil, Scottish Gaelic, means 'fort of blood'.

Ellisland Farm - Farm of Robert Burns (1759-96) from 1788 to 1791 when he gave up the lease. He built the farmhouse and outbuildings.

Finlarig Castle - is a castle built in 1629. It sits on a mound between the River Lochay and Loch Tay, about a kilometre north of the village of Killin, Perthshire, Scotland. The builder was 'Black' Duncan Campbell (Donnchadh Dubh). It is an L-shaped tower house and was once protected by a barmekin (enclosure wall). Nowadays it is a ruin. At the north wall is a pit where legend says noble prisoners were beheaded.

Finlarig House - The familial home of Raibert Mac Prainnseas Frisealach. It is situated close to the ruins of Finlarig Castle.

Finnich Glen - Stirlingshire, Scotland. It features a circular rock known as the Devil's Pulpit and a steep staircase known as the Devil's Steps, built around 1860.

Foinaven Mountain - A Scottish mountain in the north west of the Highlands within the Moine Thrust Belt. It is made up of Cambrian quartz on top of an older Lewisian gneiss basement. The summit is called Ganu Mòr. It is 2,988 feet above sea level. It is known as the sister of Arkle Mountain. It is the site of one of the vortexes that exist between the parallel worlds.

Friar's Carse - The house where Nanny worked as a young woman. Owned at the time by a Captain Robert Riddel (1755-94), Laird of Friar's Carse, a friend of Robert Burns (1759-96).

Fulham - Area in London within Borough of Hammersmith on the north bank of the River Thames.

Isle of Rùm - Island in Scotland's Inner Hebrides. Became a 'Natural Nature Reserve' in 1957, is part of the 'Small Isles National Scenic Area', and is a 'Special Area of Conservation'.

Kinlochbervie - A little village in the north west of Scotland.

Leicester - A city in the East Midlands region of England.

Lewisian Gneiss Complex - The Lewisian complex or Lewisian gneiss is a sporadic group of pre-cambrian rocks in north western Scotland.

Loch A'Garbh-Bhaid Mor - A loch in Sutherland, Scotland close to Foinaven Mountain.

Loch Assynt is a freshwater loch in Sutherland, Scotland, close to Inchnadamph.

Loch Nam Blar - A loch in Sutherland, Scotland close to Foinaven Mountain.

Lost Eagle Peak - A mountain in Wyoming, United States of America.

Part of the Wind River Range of the Rocky Mountains. The rocks is granite batholith and was formed over a billion years ago. It is the site of one of the vortexes that exist between the parallel worlds.

Milton Keynes - A large town in Buckinghamshire, England, 50 miles from London.

Moine Thrust Belt - Between Loch Eriboll to the Isle of Skye. And formed 430 million years ago when the continental plates between the countries of Scotland and England collided.

Muirkirk - A village in Ayrshire, Scotland.

New Cumnock - A village in Ayrshire, Scotland.

Priestland - Village in Irvine Valley, Ayrshire, Scotland, about 2 miles west of Loudoun Hill. Adjoins the town of Dervel.

Rosedale Abbey - A village in North Yorkshire, England around 8 miles from Pickering.

Sabhailte gu caladh reidh - Safe Haven. A defendable tower north of Foinaven Mountain. (Sixth World.)

Scotland - Alba. The land area of the Country of Scotland is 30,414 square miles and is 32% of the area known as the United Kingdom/British Isles. Scotland's mainland has 6,160 miles of coastline. It is a separate country within the United Kingdom. (Union of the Crowns of the Scots and the Crown of England, under King James VI, 1603.)

Sith Talla - Sidhe Hall. The Sixth World. This is the Cuetiachtli Training School in Scotland. (Sixth World.)

Southampton Water - Tidal estuary north of Isle of Wight, England.

Strathaven - A town in South Lanarkshire, Scotland.

Thorgill - Hamlet in Rydale, North York Moors National Park, eleven miles north west of Pickering, England.

Wyoming - The and area of the United States State of Wyoming is bordered on the north by the State of Montana, on the east by South Dakota and Nebraska, on the south by Colorado, on the southwest by Utah, and on the west by Idaho. It is the tenth largest state in the United States in total area, containing 97,814 square miles. It has no coastline. The United States Congress admitted Wyoming into the Union as the 44th State on 10th July 1890.

8. THE VORTEXES

1. Foinaven Mountain, Sutherland, Scotland. Very Intermittent. Guard numbers - small.
2. Lost Eagle Peak, Wyoming, USA. Stable most of the time. Guard numbers - large.
3. Ishpatina Ridge, Ontario, Canada. Severed/Collapsed. Guard - electronic sensors.
4. Trollaval, Isle of Rùm, Scotland. Severed/Collapsed. *
5. Kangerlusssueq, Greenland. Severed/Collapsed. Guard - sensors.
6. Kansas, mid west USA. Intermittent. Guard contingent - medium.
7. Poll Ghlup, Isle of Handa, Scotland. Stable. *
8. Inishtrahull Island, Ireland. Stable. *
9. Khibinsky Mountains, Murmansk, Russia. Severed/Collapsed. Guard - electronic sensors.

* The Faie do not know about these vortexes.

9. THE GLOSSARY

Alfred Wegener (1880-1930) - A German geologist, meteorologist and polar researcher who in 1912 proposed the theory of continental drift.

Aos Si - The Irish term for a supernatural race in Irish and Scottish mythology, known in modern times as fairies and elves.

Àrd-Righ - (Cuetiachtli (the old tongue)) & (Scottish Gaelic). High King.

Àrd-Dhia - (Cuetiachtli (the old tongue)) & (Scottish Gaelic). High God.

Army of the Faie of Alba - The army is responsible for defence and protection (primarily against Goddess Cailleach) of the landmass and islands of Britain/Britannica. It is known as 'Alba' because the fighting, 99.9% of the time, takes place in Scotland.

Army of the Faie in the Americas - The army is responsible for defence and protection (primarily against Goddess Cailleach) of the landmasses of North America and South America.

Artur (Prince) - (B: 559 - D: 594). Artuir mac Áedáin. Duke of Battles. Son of Áedáin mac Gabráin, Prince/King in Dál Riata and grandson of Gabrán mac Domangairt, King in Dál Riata.

Bairn - (Scots). Children.

Bana-phrionnsa - (Scottish Gaelic). Princess.

Banduri - A Druid word meaning female priestess. They are mentioned by Classical writers and in legend. Another name for a Priestess of the Goddess.

Bettisia Gozzadini (1209 - 61) - Probably the first woman to teach at a university.

Carse - A Scottish geographical term. 'Carse' is a modern form of Old Scots 'kerse'. It is an area of fertile, low-lying, alluvial ground that is situated along certain river valleys.

Ceannard - Commander of the Army of the Faie of Alba and therefore responsible for the protection of the landmass and islands of Britain/Britannica.

Ceithearn - (Irish Gaelic). Pronounced k-e-r-n and written as such. A band or troop of soldiers or fighting men.

Ceithernach - (Irish Gaelic) A member or a leader within a Ceithearn.

Centum - Latin word for a hundred. At Lost Eagle Peak, a centum was the word for a hundred warriors. There are 10 contubernia in a centum, making a total of 100 plus the commanding officer, the Tesserarius. Five centums usually make a legion but during periods of peril a legion can be of any size.

Clan: Chlainn - Cinneadh (m.) - Clann (f.) - Chinnidh. (Scottish Gaelic). Children. A traditional social group of families in the Scottish Highlands having a common hereditary chieftain.

Contubernium - In the Roman army this was the smallest military unit and was the size of a modern squad. It consisted of 8 legionary soldiers and two auxiliary soldiers. The American Faie military is loosely based on the Roman army. At Lost Eagle Peak, contubernium is the word used for a squad of 10. There are 10 contubernia in a centum

Crannag (Scottish Gaelic) - Crannog (English) - Crannóg (Irish). A man made island in lochs, lakes and rivers in Scotland, ireland and Wales. The majority date from the Late Bronze Age until the Early Iron Age.

Draoidh (Scottish Gaelic) - Druid (English) - Druí (Irish). In the world of the Celt they were the religious leaders, lawyers, adjudicators, tradition keepers, doctors, and advisors to Kings.

E.L.E. - Extinction Level Event.

Eyes - (Guem - yellow with a brown or black pupil) - (Bloden - a very pale blue) - (Cuetiachtli - green) - (Kobolds and Spriggans - black with white irises).

Faie in Legend - Cuetiachtli - Wolf Elves -- Fladhaich - Scottish Elves -- Siofra - Irish Elves -- Ljosalfar - Norse Elves -- Sidhe - Fairy folk --

Druas - Dryads or Tree Nymphs.

Finte of the Banduri of the Goddess - See Priestesses of Flidais.

Foinaven - (Faie - the old tongue). Alternate name for the vortex/passage/route/tunnel between parallel worlds.

Geòidh leann - Scottish Gaelic for beer keg. The Faie appropriated the name for their light, heather honey beer in the fourteenth century.

Geology - The study of rocks and how the rocks change over time. It gives insight into the history of the Earth, plate tectonics, evolution of life and climate change.

Gyre - (Scots). An evil or mischievous spirit. Phantom. Hobgoblin. Troll. Demon.

Hiding to nothing - Being faced with a pointless situation, a successful outcome being impossible.

James the Sixth, King of Scots - (B:1567 - R:1567 - D:1625). He became James the First of England in 1603.

Kelpie - A shape-shifting water sprite living in the lochs and tarns in Scotland.

Kern - (Scottish and Irish Gaelic). A soldier, a light infantryman, especially in Ireland. (Cuetiachtli (the old tongue)). Soldier. Guard-Kerns are soldiers who guard.

Lady of the Lake - An enchantress in mediaeval legend and literature relating to King Arthur. She had many names, including Nimue, Nimeuh and Nyneve.

Legionary - Soldier of the Army of the Faie in the Americas. Named after the infantryman of the Roman Army.

Lowland Scots: A Germanic language spoken in Lowland Scotland and areas of Ulster. It is often called Lowland Scots to distinguish it from Scottish Gaelic and other dialects with an English root.

Mary, Queen of Scots - (B:1542 - R:1542 - D:1587). Mother of King James the Sixth. Executed by the English Queen Elizabeth.

Muffle - A 'magical' device devised by the Goddess Flidais, thus disobeying the command of her father Jah not to interfere. It resembles a large, invisible bubble, and humans cannot see through it. The Faie use it to hide what they are doing from the general population. It is usually set in place by one or more of the Goddess's Priestesses of Flidais.

OSU - Operational Support Unit, Police Scotland. There are six of these units within the country, trained to deal with and respond to public order and CBRN (chemical, biological, radiological, nuclear) incidents.

Palaeontology - The scientific study of life that existed prior to the present day. It includes the study of fossils to determine evolution and how the creatures interacted with each other.

Praeceptolem - Army Commander of the Army of the Faie in the United States of America.

Priestesses of Flidais - A group of female Faie who have dedicated their lives to the needs of the Goddess Flidais. Also known as the Finte of the Banduri of the Goddess. Their headquarters is at Finnich Glen in Stirlingshire and known as the Teampall Gliocas.

Prionnsa - (Scottish Gaelic). Prince.

Procurator Fiscal - The local coroner and public prosecutor in Scotland. Originally an officer of the Sheriffs in Scotland who collected debts, fines and taxes. With the Criminal Procedure Act in 1701 (Scotland's Parliament) they began to prosecute in the Sheriff Court.

Ri-Beag - (Cuetiachtli (the old tongue)) & (Scottish Gaelic). Under King.

Robert the Third, King of Scots - (B:1337/40 - R:1390 - D:1406).

Teampull - (Scottish Gaelic and the Old Tongue). Temple. 'Teampall Gliocas' means 'Temple of Wisdom'.

Tesserarius - Company Commander) in the Army of the Faie in the United States of America.

Tetrad - A group of four who are trained to fight against the Kobold and the Spriggan (and anything else that threatens the Sixth world). Often two tetrads will go on missions together. Tetrads are the tradition but Weaponsmaster Zellair does not necessarily follow this route, believing that group size depends on what mission they are undertaking.

Tomahawk - A single-hand axe that came into the English Language in the seventeenth century as an adaptation of the American Algonquian Indian word for the general purpose tool, throwing or hand-to-hand weapon. The Royal Navy would have called them boarding axes.

Uilebheist - (Scottish Gaelic). Monster.

Vampire - A fictional, immortal creature from mythology. In the context of the multiverse, vampires and vampyres are often confused (by humans) with the fourth world Bloden (mixed blood of Fladhaich and a dinosaur known from the cretaceous fossil records in the sixth world as a troodon) and the Kobold (Goddess Cailleach's minions, formed by her kidnapping then adulterating the Cuetiachtli.

Vampyre - A mortal, real entity that believes that he/she needs to drink blood or absorb the energy of another person. In the context of the multiverse, vampires and vampyres are often confused (by humans) with the fourth world Bloden (mixed blood of Fladhaich and a dinosaur known from the cretaceous fossil records in the sixth world as a troodon) and the

Kobold (Goddess Cailleach's minions, formed by her kidnapping then adulterating the Cuetiachtli.

V-2 - Nazi Germany's V-2 was the world's first long-range guided ballistic missile and was powered by a liquid propellant rocket engine.

Werewolves/Conroicht/Ulfheonar/Faoladh - Guem in the context of this book. In Celtic mythology werewolves were the guardian spirits of children, wounded men and the lost. In the context of this book, werewolves come from the fifth world and are of mixed blood, Ljosalfar and Neanderthal.

Zapovjednik - Kobold army commander.

10. THE SCIENCE OF PARALLEL WORLDS

The potential that we live in a multiverse arises from a theory called eternal inflation, which says that not long after the Big Bang that formed the universe, space-time expanded at different rates in different places, giving rise to bubble universes.

The idea had been thought hypothetical but some researchers suggested that if our universe had siblings, we might have bumped into them. Such collisions would have left lasting marks in the cosmic microwave background (CMB) radiation, the diffuse light left over from the Big Bang that pervades the universe.

The existence of multiple universes – a multiverse – is therefore scientifically plausible. If all these universes emerged from the same Big Bang, then they're likely sitting together in a row, vibrating. According to the theory, if these universes touch one another, the resulting collision would leave some sort of evidence. According to New Scientist, which first reported the Dr. Chary's (Ranga-Ram Chary - U.S. Planck Data Centre at CalTech) research, this is akin to two bubbles bumping into each other. These so-called "bubble universes", which are expanding within the multiverse, bumped into each other as they expanded after the Big Bang, leaving an imprint (cosmic microwave background radiation) on each other's outer surface.

Not all scientists agree, but some - including Stephen Hawking - believe there's scientific justification for a multiverse.

There is also a possibility that a parallel world/a number of parallel worlds might be linked via the string-net liquid state phenomenon.

11. SUMMARY OF THE GEOLOGICAL TIMESCALE OF OUR PLANET EARTH

Precambrian (4,600 m.y.a. to 542 m.y.a.)
- Hadean (4,600 m.y.a. to 4,000 m.y.a.)
- Archaen (4,000 m.y.a. to 2,500 m.y.a.)
- Proterozoic (2500 m.y.a. to 542 m.y.a.)
Phanerozoic (542 m.y.a. to present)
- Paleozoic (542 m.y.a. to 251 m.y.a.)
-- Cambrian (542 m.y.a. to 488.3 m.y.a.)
-- Ordovician (488.3 m.y.a. to 443.7 m.y.a.)
-- Silurian (443.7 m.y.a. to 416 m.y.a.)
-- Devonian (416 m.y.a. to 359.2 m.y.a.)
-- Carboniferous (359.2 m.y.a. to 299 m.y.a.)
-- Permian (299 m.y.a. to 251 m.y.a.)
- Mesozoic (251 m.y.a. to 65.5 m.y.a.)
-- Triassic (251 m.y.a. to 199.6 m.y.a.)
-- Jurassic (199.6 m.y.a. to 145.5 m.y.a.)
-- Cretaceous (145.5 m.y.a. to 65.5 m.y.a.)
- Cenzoic (65.5 m.y.a. to present)
-- Paleogene (65.5 m.y.a. to 23.03 m.y.a.)
-- Neogene (23.03 m.y.a. to 2.588 m.y.a.)
-- Quatermary (2.588 m.y.a. to present)
--- Pleistocene (2.588 m.y.a. to 11,700 yrs.)
--- Holocene (11,700 yrs. to present)

12. POETS, POEMS AND QUOTES

POETS

William Dunbar (c.1459-c.1520) - Scottish makar poet. Thought to be one of Scotland's two greatest poets, the other being Robert Burns (1759-96). He has been called the Scottish Chaucer and King James the Fourth's Poet Laureate.

Robert Burns - (1759-96) - Scottish poet and songwriter. Thought to be one of Scotland's two greatest poets, the other being William Dunbar (1459-1520). He wrote in the Scots language and in English with a Scots dialect, Lallans.

Walter Scott - (1771 - 1832) - Scottish historical novelist, poet, playwright and historian.

POEMS

'TAM O'SHANTER'

When Robert Burns left Edinburgh at the beginning of 1788, he took a lease on Ellisland Farm, Dumfriesshire. He also trained as a gauger (exciseman) so he would have employment if the farm failed. There had been problems at Mossgaville (Mossgeil) Farm in Ayrshire. He took a position with the Customs and Excise in 1789 and gave up the farm in 1791. In November 1790, he wrote 'Tam O'Shanter', arguably his third most famous poem after 'Auld lang Syne' and 'To a Mouse'.

The story comes from an old legend where a Carrick farmer is drinking after a long day in the fields. As he rides home he passes the haunted Alloway Kirk. Inside are witches dancing and Old Nick himself is playing the bagpipes. The farmer sees one of the pretty witches and calls out to her with the result that the witches chase him. As it is a known 'fact' that witches cannot cross running water the farmer rides for the bride over the River Doon. He makes it, but only at the cost of his horse's tail.

> *Five tomahawks, wi blude red-rusted;*
> *Five scymitars, wi' murder crusted.*

(English translation: wi - with --- blude - blood --- scymitars - scimitars.)

> *The wind blew as 'twad blawn its last;*
> *The rattling showers rose on the blast;*
> *The speedy gleams the darkness swallow'd,*
> *Loud, deep, and lang, the thunder bellow'd:*
> *That night, a child might understand,*
> *The Deil had business on his hand.*

(English translation: as 'twad blawn - as if it had blown --- deep, and lang - deep and long ---The Deil - The Devil.)

> *So Maggie runs, the witches follow,*
> *Wi' mony an eldritch skriech and hollo.*

(English translation: Wi' mony an eldritch skriech and hollo - With many an unearthly scream and holler.)

The lightnings flash from pole to pole;
Near and more near the thunders roll.

(English translation: not required.)

"While we sit bousing at the nappy,
And getting fou and unco happy.

(English translation: bousing - boozing --- nappy - strong ale --- fou - drunk --- unco - very.)

'AULD LAND SYNE'

There are a number of versions of this famous poem and song, not all of which, for obvious reasons, can be attributed to Robert Burns.

Auld Lang Syne can be translated to 'old long since' or perhaps 'long long ago'. Therefore, the translation can be stretched to say 'for the sake of auld lang syne'.

Robert Burns sent a copy of the original song to the Scots Musical Museum with the comment, 'The following song, an old song, of the olden times, and which has never been in print, nor even in manuscript until I took it down from an old man.' In the ballad 'Old Long Syne' printed in 1711 by James Watson there are similarities in the first verse and the chorus to the later poem of Robert Burns, and is almost certainly derived from the same 'old song'.

BANNATYNE MANUSCRIPT OF 1568 (AULD KYNDNES FORYETT)

They wald me hals with hude and hatt, Quhyle I wes rich and had
anewch,
About me friends anew I gatt, Rycht blythlie on me they lewch;
But now they mak it wondir tewch, And lattis me stand befoir the yett;
Thairfoir this warld is very frewch, And auld kyndnes is quyt foryett.

ROBERT AYTON (1570-1638)

Should auld acquaintance be forgot and never thought upon,
The flames of love extinguished and freely past and gone?
Is thy kind heart now grown so cold in that loving breast of thine,
That thou canst never once reflect on old-long-syne?
On old long syne, my Jo, on old long syne,
That thou canst never once reflect on old long syne.

FRANCIS SEMPILL OF BELTREES (d.c.1683) (ATTRIB)

On old long syne.
On old long syne, my jo, On old long syne:
That thou canst never once reflect, On old long syne.

ALLAN RAMSAY (1684 - 1743)

Should auld acquaintance be forgot, Tho' they return with scars?
These are the noble hero's lot, Obtain'd in glorious wars:
Welcome, my Varo, to my breast, Thy arms about me twine.
And make me once again as blest, As I was lang syne.

ROBERT BURNS (1759-96)

Should auld acquaintance be forgot, and never brought to mind?
Should auld acquaintance be forgot, and auld lang syne?
And surely ye'll be your pint-stoup! And surely I'll be mine!
And we'll tak' a cup o' kindness yet, for auld lang syne.
We twa hae run about the braes, and pou'd the gowans fine;
But we've wander'd mony a weary fit, sin' auld lang syne.
We twa hae paidl'd in the burn, frae morning sun till dine;
But seas between us braid hae roar'd sin' auld lang syne.
And there's a hand, my trusty fiere! And gie's a hand o' thine!
And we'll tak' a right gude-willie waught, for auld lang syne.
For auld lang syne, my jo, for auld lang syne,
We'll tak' a cup o' kindness yet, for auld lang syne.

NURSERY RHYMES

Tommy Thumb's Pretty Song Book is the earliest surviving collection of nursery rhymes. It was first printed in London in 1744. No first editions have survived but there were a number of reprints.ered from later reprints. It contained many rhymes that are familiar to today's children. The author is a 'Nurse Lovechild'.

1744 Version - *Sing a Song of Sixpence, A bag full of Rye, Four and twenty Naughty Boys, Baked in a Pye.* Today's version - Sing a song of sixpence, A pocket full of rye, Four and twenty blackbirds, Baked in a pie.

1744 Version - Little Robin Red breast, Sitting on a pole, Nidde,

Noddle, Went his head. And poop went his Hole. Today's version - Little Robin Redbreast, Sat upon a rail; Niddle noble went his head, Widdle waggle went his tail.

1744 Version - Ride a cock-horse, To Banbury Cross, To see what Tommy can buy; A penny white loaf, A penny white cake, And a two-penny apple-pie. Today's version - Ride a cock-horse to Banbury Cross, To see a fine lady upon a white horse; Rings on her fingers and bells on her toes, And she shall have music wherever she goes.

QUOTES

'Gie a bairn his will and whelp his fill, and neither will dae weel' - Scottish saying - 'Spare the rod and spoil the child'.

"Give thine ears, hear the words that are said, give thine heart to interpret them." - Instruction of Amenomope, from Ancient Egyptian wisdom text composed during the Ramesside Period (1300 to 1075 BC).

13. ACKNOWLEDGEMENTS

*almanac.com
*cairnwater.co.uk
*biology-online.org/dictionary.com
*hannover.park.org.
*hymnsandcarolsofchristmas.com
*earthsky.org.
*oldebible.com (1560 - Translation - Geneva Bible)
*robertburns.org.uk
*space.com.
*thebottleimp.co.uk
*wikipedia.com.
*jncc.defra.gov.uk/pdf/V34Chap1.pdf.
*io9.gizmodo.com/the-one-basic-fact-about-history-that-time-travelers-always-forget.
*Scottish Customs: From the Cradle to the Grave - Margaret Bennett. (Birlinn Ltd, New edition, 2011)
*The Poetic Edda: Translated by Carolyne Larrington. (Oxford University Press - 2014).
*Research paper in Earth and Planetary Science Letters. Louis Bergeron, Stanford News Service.
*A Dictionary of the Gaelic Language: In Two Parts - (Norman

Macleod (1831)).

*Dictionarium Scoto-Celticum: a Dictionary of the Gaelic Language - (Published by William Blackwood, Edinburgh (1828)).

*Folk Tales and Fairy Lore in Gaelic and English - Rev. James MacDougall - (Published by John Grant, Edinburgh (1910)).

*Scotch Presbyterian Eloquence Display'd - Gilbert Crokatt and John Monro - (First published in London 1694 by Randal Taylor near Stationers-Hall) (Van Anker Edition - 1738).

ABOUT THE AUTHOR

Candy Rae lives in Ayrshire, Scotland with her dog Alex and a cat, Sammy who thinks he is the boss of the house. She has been a fan of fantasy fiction (and sci-fi as long as it isn't too technical) since her first year at university when a friend introduced her to talking dragons.

She started to write one Christmas Day when she sat down and planned her first book, which, after many revisions, became the first book in the Planet Wolf Series, Wolves and War.

Candy Rae used to work in accountancy where she scribbled down words in amongst the figures. She carries a notebook everywhere she goes into which she writes down her ideas. She has been known to drive off the motorway, park the car in the first available spot and write for an hour or more.